The Theory of Fun
and Other Stories

Stephen Conrad

Grosvenor House
Publishing Limited

This book is published by
Grosvenor House Publishing Ltd
Link House
140 The Broadway, Tolworth, Surrey, KT6 7HT.
www.grosvenorhousepublishing.co.uk

This book is a work of fiction. Any resemblance to
people or events, past or present, is purely coincidental.

A CIP record for this book
is available from the British Library

ISBN 978-1-83615-414-3

For CP, who always encouraged,
and PC, who insisted.

And for my father,
who understands myth.

Contents

No Thunderbolts

1

She should never have called him indecisive. That was asking for trouble. It was then that he decided to end her. She had at least done better than the others, had lasted a while before driving him once again to destruction. So, with one decisive blow, this brief courtship had ended. For the best. It's all for the best in the end.

The first one had been more straightforward: a snaggle-toothed hag who had, in her soft-focus picture, been draped horizontally across an armchair, wearing an unbuttoned cowgirl shirt. Vaguely reminiscent of a '40s film poster which had caused a stir at the time. In real life, she'd been somewhat less alluring than Jane Russell. Most people are.

After an initial exchange, along the lines of, "God, you're posh, you're so posh!" they had sat on a park bench shivering to death. He detested being called posh because he wasn't remotely. He was simply well read, confident, and therefore well-spoken. He had not been to private school and tended to despise anyone who had, whilst at the same time enjoying the dismissive, languorous, essentially 'English' manner that it seemed to engender on occasion. (At least among the wittier, more erudite attendees of such establishments.) It was clearly impossible and ludicrous to despise the likes of Orwell, Waugh and Huxley, but he often wondered how they would have fared without the privilege. Orwell, you imagine, would have fared exactly the same.

They had sat on the bench shivering to death because she was fiercely independent and would rely on no man for money. He hadn't offered her money, merely a coffee. But even this was too vast a gesture of patronage. Her fierce independence did not, it seemed, prevent her from accepting her ex-husband's mortgage payments. These were not actually useful because they did not represent cash in hand. For that she had to rely on handouts from the government, towards which she evinced an unflinching sense of entitlement. Though very critical of people who did nothing to help themselves, who apparently sat around all day drinking lager, it was not at all clear what she herself did. Sat around all day *not* drinking lager presumably. She couldn't work because she had a debilitating disease. It was in remission most of the time, but she didn't know when it would strike. He had no idea what the disease was because she didn't want it to 'define her'; a phrase she had perhaps picked up watching daytime television. He suggested that maybe she could work between bouts of this unpredictable disease, but evidently not. Perhaps the inflexibility of the benefits system did indeed shackle this repressed titan of industry. In any case, she had to go. She had to go quickly.

*

Joseph Storm was rather prone to insignificant gestures of grandeur; he tended to mythologize both himself and others. His noble timing and way of organising his actions were based on a sense of order, of epic propriety. Even the most loathsome acts could be performed with a certain solemnity. Once he had convinced himself he was right, which was most of the time, he managed to construct a sense of narrative around his behaviour. A logical sequence which, given certain starting assumptions, was technically correct and which salved his conscience. In fact, his thinly disguised need to control every aspect of his existence made a poor impression on those around him. His gestures were far less impressive than he imagined. His flippant manner was strained, and his disparaging approach belied a need to do the right thing; to be *seen* to be doing the right thing. And, more importantly, to make those around him behave as they should. He was of course doomed to fail in that regard. No matter how hard you try, you can't make other people behave as they should.

He had been damaged, like many of us, by a sequence of events that weren't entirely of his own choosing. On the few occasions when he had acted out of character, when he had fallen short of the high standards he set for himself, things had ended badly. There had been things of which he was not proud, mistakes which should have been corrected earlier; there were embarrassing blemishes on his largely flawless moral record. He liked to think of himself as relaxed but in fact was not. He was haunted by things that somehow he should have controlled.

*

The second encounter had been initially more promising – a dark-haired, sneering contemporary who met him in a bar. They had discussed childhood programs, boredom, going to pubs, and having lazy weekends. It turned out that he was not her type. As a rule, she preferred military sorts with a swaggering gait and limited horizons. (She had a muscle-headed ex-boyfriend who had evidently left various scars.) There was a certain native wit about her, and she wasn't used to meeting strangers like this – taking a chance on love. She hadn't met anyone quite like him before, nor would she again.

Then came the walrus who, for a while, was his last victim. She had described herself as curvaceous in the sales patter, and this was true. She was one long curve, a rubbery, sweating pustule with a face like blancmange. The mere fact she allowed herself the light of day was a testament to her strength of character. She hobbled around on high heels as if auditioning for a supporting role in *Cinderella*.

In an effort to appear sophisticated, she had mentioned that she liked classical music. So, he'd played her at her own game and taken her to an evening of Birtwistle in a provincial concert hall. It was of course excruciating and, as such, matched her appearance admirably. To make matters worse, she had insisted on blowing her nose every 15 seconds, emitting a little high-pitched "eek" at the end of each meek sneeze. Christ, it had been insufferable.

She droned through a list of her previous encounters and even described her last boyfriend. It was as if she needed to prove that she'd managed to spend an evening with someone who hadn't hurled himself through a window just to escape the horror. By her account at least, her last boyfriend was an insensate oaf who hadn't wanted children. She clearly did, as a matter of some urgency, and Joseph wondered if next time he might not be better served just bringing along a bag of semen: "There you are, hopefully it will work out. Let me know if you need any more."

Really, this dating game was becoming a chore. He had emerged from the proverbial wreckage of his divorce some years ago. This had been a tawdry affair to begin with, but then, in the end, relatively civilised, once lawyers and other parasitic vermin were dispensed with. In fact, he came to realise that the only people who had acted with dignity throughout had been himself and his ex-wife. There was not a day went by that he didn't wonder what on earth they had been thinking.

4

The unoriginality of it all appalled him. It remained a failure, a canker in his uncompromising view of how things should be. It undermined his sense of integrity. Rather than fix things, they had shored up for a while. His sense of humour, unfailing, had provided brief glimpses of the future; her beauty, still overwhelming, had provided brief glimpses of the past. But they hadn't protected each other. He had not managed the situation – he had allowed things to slip out of his control, and then, well, then it became too far to go back. Most worthwhile journeys don't bear repeating.

Despite believing he wanted to be alone, that he was unsuited to womankind, he had begun to get lonely. Lonely, desperate men with their pitiful little urges: mythologize that if you can. He had signed up to a lonely-hearts service, or rather the modern equivalent. Setting his selection parameters generously wide, he had begun searching for like-minded losers: unmarried, slim, aged 32–45; preferably not a strict vegetarian. So far, so bad.

After the walrus came the googly-eyed, psychotic psychologist. The start of the affair was an inauspicious test of patience, when a mix up over the agreed meeting place meant that they sat at opposite ends of a stone cloister for 20 minutes. Joseph pondered becoming a monk – lounging around all day making mead sounded all right. Tensions were eased by a farcical routine of apology and mistaken location debate, followed by forced laughter. They then launched into silence.

She wandered around rose bushes with him for a while, then they went to a café and ate a salad of some description. She didn't say much, and he'd assumed that she was used to listening. Unfortunately, he didn't say much either and so any analysis was fairly difficult, at best qualitative. He had not been shrunk.

He abhorred small talk. Because he wasn't any good at it, he had decided it was fake and pretentious drivel, rather than the essential social tool it actually was. His manner of small talk was to stare fixedly at someone for hours then make a gauche remark, if drunk enough. It had worked on one memorable occasion, when the woman concerned had been quite bowled over with surprise. He'd been trying to look smouldering and Byronic – she'd assumed he wanted to kill her.

Unfortunately, the most interesting thing about that date had been the cucumber. He'd sent a courtesy note along the lines of 'Lovely to meet you but no thunderbolts', which had occasioned an unusually belligerent response – something about being shallow and judgemental. He'd assumed she was referring to someone else. His view was that people were not judgemental enough. There was a right and a wrong. It was as simple as that.

Joseph was in some sense a decent man, but he took himself, and life, too seriously. He could only see one way of approaching things; could only deal with one set of perceived circumstances at a time. He could not bear his routine or, in particular, his environment, to be altered. Change was not to be borne at any cost. And yet his penchant for self-destruction sometimes devoured him. It was as if all the small, inconsequential changes that he railed so violently against were somehow stored up and magnified. Eventually, resistance broke down and lay discarded. He could never embrace change; he had to be engulfed by it.

Most women he'd come across in this adventure were either repulsive or so desperate to have children, like the walrus, that it was simply embarrassing. It was almost as if he were being measured and interviewed as a potential donor, regardless of any other considerations. Most stopped short of requesting a full medical history, but it certainly upheld his previous belief that it was not only men who objectified the opposite sex; feminists needed to sort out their own corner as well.

Other brief encounters had included a manic Catholic on speed; a woman who appeared interested in tennis and nothing else; a rock chick who naturally liked motorbikes and had made him feel wholly lacking in butch machismo, and a Mafia moll. The latter had bizarrely phoned him from a plane just to hear his voice. She seemed to have lots of brothers, a white streak in her hair, and spoke with an Italian accent. There was something terrifying about her casualness. He had also browsed past an old schoolfriend who, unbelievably, was holding a bassoon in her profile picture! Perhaps wanting to indicate how good she was with wood.

His penultimate meeting had been with a nymphomaniac vampire druid. Somehow, she had appeared staggeringly attractive in her picture, with cheeks sucked in, pitch-black hair, and backlighting and mascara that made her eyes seem the size of saucers. In real life she was a daubed-up fiend with no sense of dressing for her age or considerable size. However, she was at least garrulous and had a no-nonsense manner of address that held a certain dominant fascination. She had talked about vaguely pagan inclinations and being close to nature.

It had been a long time, and he had been mildly enthusiastic in his feedback, but after a fortnight she had sent him a reply with the usual 'nice to see you, not my type' couplet. He had replied, with the necessarily unruffled, "No problem, hope it works out for you," but then for some reason, added, "Let me know if you fancy a fling!" This was not remotely in his compass, but then his compass had been slightly without direction for some time. It was badly in need of realignment.

Bizarrely, she had replied with, "That sounds like fun, I've been feeling really horny lately! Where shall we meet?"

This had actually happened. This was how some people ran their lives and, perhaps, they were happier for it. Joseph had run a mile and indeed was still running. He'd had visions of being lured to a field on summer solstice before being sacrificed in front of a crowd of heathens chanting praises to the devil. On reflection, this was a blinkered response, and he rather regretted his inaction. It could have opened up a whole new arena. But he had never been young and uninhibited; he'd never been interested in, nor capable of, flings. Nor indeed the frenetic chaos that surrounded them. For him, love was supposed to be played out in a certain, if limited, way.

None of these encounters went beyond the vertical.

*

That only left the final instalment of his short quest for companionship, which had ended so abruptly. Nothing really ends abruptly, of course – first it has to rot. He'd spent the last year or so with a landscape gardener called Beatrice, whose hobbies included knitting, making marmalade and photography. She had lots of friends, and he should probably have been added to that less intimate list, rather than the somewhat shorter list of people she'd been to bed with. No one had been hurt, or at least he hoped not.

Leaving someone for calling you indecisive seemed a reasonable thing to do. He had once left somebody because they read the

Daily Mail and, on another occasion, returned home early from a weekend away because his travelling companion ate too loudly. He had tried the traditional male approach of behaving like a boorish, apathetic sociopath until his partner grew tired of him. Unfortunately, Beatrice had rather more staying power than he was expecting, and so in the end he had made his excuses and exited stage left. It was always a matter of finding an excuse.

The problem was that love, like spontaneity, was a youthful pursuit. Being with someone was about forging a future, building a life. He now had a life, crumbling and vacated though it was. His marriage had failed and, therefore, in some way he felt that he could not return to married life or any semblance of it; as if beginning again would somehow undermine his original rapture. Joseph was more concerned with preservation than development, more concerned with the past than with the present. He had his rich life (albeit now much reduced), and he had his pleasures, both simple and profound. It was inconceivable that a stranger, without shared history, could add meaningfully to that.

If nothing else, his brief foray into the world of small talk had shown him that loneliness was preferable to debating the weather. Misery was better than the slovenly detritus of others. Control was more important than joy.

He had a routine. He was a bureaucracy of one.

2

If he'd arrived any earlier, it would have been yesterday. His Soulmates account had still been open and through sheer stubbornness he was having one last throw of the dice. He'd been practising his shaking action, and the motion was now second nature. In fact, he and a work colleague had briefly considered launching a backgammon based dating site called 'Roller' but decided it was too niche.

He glanced around the restaurant for no good reason except that he was bored of the fork. There was a couple across the room who were either on a bad first date or a good first divorce one. She wasn't so much rolling her eyes upwards as gluing her eyelids to the back of her skull. He couldn't see the male face in the equation but, statistically, she was likely to be well out of his league. Not that such leagues exist, apparently, or so say those who, like him, resided in the lower divisions. Lower-middle, let's be kind. Hopefully, his own evening's entertainment would be as visually appealing. He wasn't shallow, but hidden depths had to lap the shore somewhere.

*

"So yes, there are three different indigenous cedar trees in the UK."

She'd have quite happily lived out her whole life without knowing that and therefore immediately forgot it. The same was true of this entire so-called date. Friend of a friend for heaven's sake. Time to re-evaluate that acquaintance. Maybe it had been a wind up. It was inconceivable that anyone could think this living yawn sitting opposite her was anything other than a colossal monument to tedium. She didn't want to be unkind, but the fact that he was allegedly 'such a nice guy' was both largely irrelevant and patently untrue. Nice guys don't destroy you with arboreal anecdotes within half an hour of appearing.

"The Atlas cedar, the cedar of Lebanon and the Deodar."

"Right. Well, as I say, I like how they spread."

"Sorry, I'm being a colossal monument to tedium."

"Not at all!"

The mansplaining exercise nut should just fuck off and be a lumberjack if he liked trees so much. Besides which, he seemed to have most of a tree stuck in his teeth. This must be a wind up. She wasn't about to go running, or cycling, wrapped up in a giant spandex condom, or bungee jumping. *Grow up, you nob*! Just moving was fine, moving was plenty. Life was too short for exercise. In a sudden burst of energy, she stood up.

"I just need to pop out for a minute, won't be long. Must be nerves!"

*

Joseph was having a fairly bad time. She had turned up late and failed to hide her disappointment at his average appearance, despite the fact he had been almost entirely honest in his advert. She had not. The evening was clearly going to be a disaster, or at least a disappointment. (If no one died, it wasn't a disaster.) Was it worth making the best of things, or would it be simpler (if ruder) and cheaper to just call it a day after one glass of 'I'll just have tonic water please, I'm driving'? Fun, fun, fun.

He wondered whether tonic water was still used to treat malaria. Probably not. He'd rather catch malaria than be sitting here.

Wrenching his mind back to the situation in hand, he noticed that his date had an appalling habit of sucking air in to cool her food down while it was hovering outside her mouth, then doing a kind of 'slurp' while it lingered in the entrance hall of her gob, before journeying to the internal sewer. It was a bit like the last few seconds of scummy bathwater gurgling down a plughole. To make matters worse, she also scraped her spoon across her teeth as she dragged it out of her mouth.
Blow on it, you piggy whore! he thought.

At least, he didn't think he'd enunciated it – the lack of response from his meal mate suggested that his own manners at least were intact, while hers descended further into the lower circles of Hell. After finger-picking her way through the chicken goujons, she proceeded to lick herself. It was his considered opinion that anyone who licked their own fingers clean in public deserved to have them cut off. He wondered whether only having your fingers cut off would be much better than whole hands – you'd still be able to clap and carry certain objects. (Although you could carry burning braziers between your forearms easily enough so maybe that wasn't such an advantage.) You wouldn't be able to drum your fingers, but you could pat. Some kind of glove might be in order.

"Sorry, I was slightly distracted. Appallingly rude."

She hadn't noticed him being slightly distracted because she was playing with her mobile phone. It was his considered opinion that people who played with their mobile phone during a first date should have it shoved up their arse. Unless it was answering the demands of children of course – they get to break all the rules.

"Excuse me a moment."

If she was busy surfing, then he could fake a toilet break. It was fake because his bladder was roughly the size of a cathedral to Saint Urine. He'd mostly given up smoking these days, but as he passed the inviting lure of the outside door, he decided fresh air was the thing.

*

"Yes?"

"Er, oh sorry, I didn't mean to stare – bad habit."

She stood outside the restaurant flicking ash from a small cigar. It was the most unlikely thing he'd ever seen.

"I don't suppose you're got one going spare, have you? Sorry to ask."

"Well, you're not sorry are you, or you wouldn't have."

There is a certain vague camaraderie amongst smokers, lapsed or otherwise. Generally, they are happy to share and not embarrassed to ask. The Cancer Club is highly inclusive.

"I don't really smoke any more."

"No, me neither," she said, taking a long drag.

"I'm having a fairly poor first date."

She flicked across the tin. "I've had better."

As with all cigar tins now, there was a picture on the front of some alarming health prognosis. He'd much preferred it when they just had a cup of coffee and a waft of burning ember. They might as well change the brand name to Café Phlegm.

"Oh thanks, great. I can't stand these new pictures of rotting toes and gaping neck holes. As if I don't know."

"It's health and safety gone mad."

He extracted a small cigar with a certain ease of familiarity and handed back her box. He considered rolling it between fingers next to his ear or smelling it. But mercifully thought better of doing so.

"I don't suppose I can borrow your light as well?"

She rolled her eyes again. "Do you have lips!"

Joseph smiled and then reminded himself why smoking is actually fairly great at times.

"Thank you. I'm Joe."

"Of course you are. I'm Fridya."

"That's unusual."

"Not in Sweden."

"Are you Swedish, then?"

"No."

He'd never quite had a conversation like this.

"My father liked artistic eyebrows and Teutonic myths – my name was something of a compromise. It could have been worse: we had a cat called Frigg."

He wasn't sure if they were smirting or not, but it was enjoyable puffing.

"I had to sneak out – my health freak lump of dating material certainly wouldn't approve," said Fridya.

"Surely you didn't lie in your profile about being a non-smoker?"

"Of course not. If anything, I talked myself down. As you can see, I'm gorgeous. But this was an arranged miscarriage. Definitely a wind up."

Joseph had really had enough of pretence. Life was indeed too short for cycling around. From now on, he'd be impulsive.

"Do you fancy a drink somewhere else?"

She paused for roughly an eternity and then answered without turning: "Why not, can't be any worse!"
This was high praise indeed. It might even go to his head.

"What about them inside?" he gestured vaguely.

"Oh, they'll work it out. Maybe they will find each other. Hang on a second."

Fridya reappeared a second later.

"All sorted. The waiter was happy to oblige; he has a sense of the ridiculous. If they don't get on, then I'll settle up tomorrow. You can be called away on urgent business."

"I'm a statistician."

"OK, then you can lie."

They smoked off into the night.

Gong

It was just a big cymbal. But it was also a symbol, of epic
proportions. It was a punitive pun, a mountain beaten flat. It
represented thunder and turmoil, a colossal pounding at the
door of fate! Whatever else, she had to hit it hard and not fuck
up. The problem with playing percussion in an orchestra was
that everyone else thought you were shit. Generally speaking,
you were. There is truth in the old joke: 'What do you call
someone who hangs around with musicians?' A drummer. Fine.
Funny. She wondered what Buddy Rich's reaction would have
been to that joke. She doubted anyone had ever cracked it
around him. But in any case, at least people knew what a
drummer was. No one knew what a percussionist was. 'What do
you call someone who hangs around with drummers?' A what?

At least a gong was big. Fuck you, triangle boy. So what if her
friends had asked her if she liked playing the dong. This one
was huge. It was as big as the one at the start of Rank films,
with greased-up Gongman. She'd not realised until recently that
the organisation was British, named after its founder J. Arthur
Rank. Daft name. Maybe even dafter than her own. Perhaps she
would take her shirt off and grease up before her big moment. It
might wake the audience up. The majority were there under
some duress because, after all, this was a school concert. Most
school concerts are unremittingly, without question, execrable.
You'd rather go and listen to a cat being sawn in half than
endure a primary school recorder concert. However, this was at
the far distant end of the spectrum – a county youth orchestra
no less, containing only the cream of young talent. Behind the

huge orchestra there was also a choir (for the less talented – the curds of young talent). Students who had gone on to university were allowed to stay in the orchestra until they graduated, which also lent a certain level of maturity to proceedings. The older members were expected to show a good example to the minions, which they mostly did by avoiding them.

Back then, in the mid-'80s, Suffolk still had a great tradition of free music in state schools, supported by the beautiful epicentre of Snape Maltings, which had strong links with the county music school in Ipswich. It had pissed from a great height on Norfolk, its more desolate neighbour. Things were different now, with successive governments utterly failing to promote and support state school music for 40-odd years. A travesty. You'd expect the Tories to crush the state sector, but Labour hadn't really been much better. They were crap for the arts. Much better to learn how to play a laptop than a clarinet; much better for only wealthy people to play classical music, rather than the ignorant masses.

But anyway, this was then and not now! Let's avoid the politics. Back to the gong.

Daisy Lampwort was struggling to concentrate. She tended to drift at the best of times, but there is so little to do in the percussion section that it's genuinely quite hard to stay focussed. It's even worse than playing the trumpet in a Mozart symphony, which is itself an odyssey of boredom. Here are a million bars rest to count before you come in and play one note. Try not to nod off. The conductor won't even bring you in half the time. It felt like he was more likely to wander over and bring you off given his lecherous side remarks: "Strong wrists, please, a useful thing in a woman!" And so on. As such, her mind kept wandering around the crotchets. Why on earth was she stuck in the percussion section? The answer was obvious: she played the piano. She wasn't quite good enough to bash out a full concerto in public, and, apart from that, there is very little call for tinkling ivory in a symphony hall. But, to add insult to injury, the piece they were performing *did* have a piano part. And not just one but two!

She didn't mind Ruth Jenkins playing, she was truly gifted and deserved her place. She was quite good enough to bash out a full concerto in public, one of the easier ones anyway. Whether she'd make it, who knew. It was probably harder to be a professional musician than a professional tiddlywinks player. 10% talent, 90% hard work, as a lovely old teacher of hers called Tom was fond of saying. But good looks and good luck seemed just as important. Such was life: no one wants to see a face like a slapped arse up on the stage. Ruth's face didn't look like a slapped arse, or even an un-slapped one – she was porcelain pretty. But not Toby Snuffle, he was a snivelling little turd! He had no business being there, taking her place. The bastard should have been on bongos. The only reason he'd been picked for the second piano was because he was the brown-nosed nephew of the cello teacher, Miss Pineapple. Bollocks to him, she hoped he screwed it up, or the lid accidentally got slammed down hard onto his jammy, wank-sticky fingers.

So, she was consigned to the percussion section, one beat away from oblivion. It was nerve-shredding, at times. On a previous occasion, she had stood up for a rare cymbal clash with only the vaguest clue where she was in the music. That's an uncomfortable place to be. Standing poised, crucified into position like a wind-up monkey, waiting for the glorious moment of release when all else was shattered. She missed her entry. The horror of exposure, the scarlet invasion of humiliation. The conductor, who was at least partly to blame, had glowered at her as if she'd just taken a dump on his podium. She had lowered the cymbals and made as if to adjust a wing nut on the stand. That could not happen again.

Carmina Burana is a magnificent piece, and putting something of this scale on with an amateur orchestra was quite a feat. It is often regarded with scorn by 'serious' classical music fans because it is popular. Serious classical music snobs, whom we shall call the snorts, look down on popular classical music because it is lowbrow. They dismiss such music as approachable, or lightweight. Why music shouldn't be approachable is a mystery. The snorts, for instance, revile the use of classical music in TV adverts because it lessens the composer's vision. That of course is nonsense – most composers would quite happily have flogged their music to whoever paid the most. They scoff at film music because it doesn't have four movements, even though some of it is wondrous. Beethoven would certainly be writing film scores if he was still alive! The snorts really have it in for the rest of us. They'd rather listen to violins being played behind the bridge, or cats being sawn in half. Not very approachable.

Like the *New World Symphony* (second movement aka the Hovis tune), *Carmina Burana* is packed full of great tunes. Great tunes aren't enough of course, if you're a snort, but they're a good start. Criticise something for being too melodic if you like or get a life. Despite her own modest contribution, Daisy thought the music was fantastically immodest. She had little to no idea about the bawdy monastic stories upon which it was based, but gorging, boozing and shagging seemed to be the order of the day. Appropriately, as well as being full of tunes, the piece was also rammed with rhythmic intensity. The composer had deliberately used repetitive patterns and avoided excessive harmonic complexity. What you heard was what you got. She wondered whether he had a sister called Fark.

In contrast to this simplicity, the vast scale of orchestration included all kinds of bizarre musical combinations. There isn't a lot of other repertoire for horn and contrabassoon. Some of the songs were as rapturous as their medieval lyrics. Disregarding literal interpretations of 'bending to the yoke' by overly enthusiastic language students, *In Trutina* was simply a gorgeous soprano aria. Anyone who hadn't heard Lucia Popp do it was missing out. Daisy had picked up titbits like this from CD sleeves during the innumerable idle hours of her first-year university course. Album notes were a great source of ad hoc information. About a decade later, pompous Classic FM presenters would get paid to read them out, as if somehow founts of all knowledge.

From start to finish, the piece was a ripper. As well as sins of the flesh, the grand entrance and exit music had something to do with fate. *O Fortuna* itself, the bombastic main theme, was certainly good enough to be reprised at the end. What goes around comes around. Destiny is like that.

*

Kenneth Brown sat in the 20th row. His wife had dragged him to this gig on the lure of its music being used in the Old Spice advert. Good advert, he couldn't argue with that, although he was more of a Brut man himself. He was also more of a saving-it-up-for-a-Saturday-night kind of guy. Classical music was for poofs, as far as he could tell. And jazz was even worse! What the fuck was that all about? Still, nothing ventured, and hopefully it would keep her sweet. He was open-minded, to a degree. Of course he'd heard the odd snippet, but somehow didn't associate it with classical music as such. There was something horribly exclusive about these places, something puny and prim. Rock and classical didn't mix, not in his book. Jon Lord and Malcom Arnold would disagree of course, as would Roger Waters. Be that as it may.

These particular Browns had not had children of their own, for various reasons he didn't like to dwell upon. Something to do with plumbing – his or hers. Doctors were about as much use as a cactus cock. People only had children to perpetuate themselves anyway; it was a supremely unoriginal self-indulgence. So, none of their own spawn were present, but they had a niece huddled among the second violins. She *would* play a musical instrument of course: his smug prick of a brother-in-law was aspirational.

Amid the frantic bowing, the howling and wailing of woodwind, brass and choir, was there something more in all of this? The conductor looked like a dickhead with his tails, the primped up fuckpig. He might be able to fool a bunch of fannying kids, but he'd like to see him in charge of a rugby team. Or running the village pigeon fanciers' group. That took real leadership. That was a bloodbath. Not least the time that Fred had groped Dave's wife and been locked in the shed, while Dave had a go at re-enacting the final scene in *Kes*. The vicar had intervened, briefly displaying his man-of-peace credentials. Anyway, he might as well listen since he was here. Suddenly, the trombones piled into another tune he recognised. Engine oil or a car, he couldn't recall. Good though, a decent tune.

Daisy was getting there, heading towards her moment of glory. She started counting: one, two, three, four, two, two, three, four, three, two, three, four. And so on. Concentration: the bane of the free. The first number was the number of bars, the next three numbers, the beats. Only three or four beats normally, unless you were some modern weirdo. No strict need to count really because her gong cataclysm came just after the previous section. But it was a quick segue. No time for messing around picking up the stick, this was one shaft that could not be dropped.

Balls! Was that 30 or 32 bars? Arse! Percussion parts were essentially impossible to follow, like Morse code, or slug shit all over the page. So no use checking the triangle boy's part. She glanced down at the horn parts below her, mercifully annotated with large letters. They were bellowing away in the row in front, and she could make out the right passage. That was fine, she was back in the groove. Ha! Good job she was a proper musician and not just a meathead.

She took a deep breath and moved the beater back, arms behind her now. There could be no more breathing until the job was done. With the focus of an Olympic hammer thrower, the grace of a ballerina and a heart of stone she began her descent. The weapon scythed through the air, as ruthless as death. Time faltered, there was nothing left in all the world. This had to be the right place. Fully extended, leaning back into the stroke, she closed her eyes and let it happen.

A wall of sound, a crashing tsunami enveloped the auditorium. A collective shudder followed the frenzied foreplay of anticipation. No one there would ever forget it – no one would ever try to. Daisy felt a juddering ripple of impact careering through her; her right shoulder tensed with the strain. As the self-induced thunderclap engulfed her, she was hurled into her own private storm. The typhoon of her future harnessed. Fuck you, man! She nailed it. It had been her moment, an all-conquering moment of glory. In many ways, she never topped this moment, but then she never needed to.

Daisy's father was in the audience. They'd both been through a lot, with one thing and another. Dark times but also light. He knew what this would mean to his daughter. Parents are essentially helpless witnesses once the spinning top gets released. But this was a prize, a day to treasure. For years it would be taken out of its trove, passed around and marvelled over.

What was wrong with living on past glories? We must endure enough past failures so a few glories don't go amiss. Remembering ever-receding moments of perfection is what anchors us to hope. Without hope, reality is unbearable. Regardless of bed mate, we all sleep alone.

It doesn't mean that everything else is appalling, just not as good as the best times. In dotage, sitting in front of *Antiques Roadshow* in your own shit is *not* as good as witnessing the birth of your first child! By definition we live out an average life, relative to ourselves. My big deal isn't for you. Hands off. Unless you're deluded or arrogant enough to compare yourself to other people, the issue of whether your life is richer than theirs is a matter of infinite boredom.

Do you remember, do I remember? Of course we do. It is all we have. When memories crumble away, they surely take us with them.

Kenneth Brown said nothing to his wife. He let out a long, slow sigh.

The Dog Walker

1

I'd not met the dog walker before and suspect I never will again. Just before the accident we held a brief conversation. That was an accident in itself, or at least a mistake. It was one of those one-way affairs, where I found myself repeating over and over again the same bored phrase into glazed, uncomprehending eyes. This usually occurs after several years of acquaintance and I imagine is how most people spend their lives, but this time it happened almost instantaneously.

A white husky had been running around outside the house. I'm roughly the same height as an Eskimo, so this came as no surprise to me. Presumably it recognised some kindred spirit of ancient ownership. Most of my friends call me Quinn. Funny. Fortunately, I don't have many friends. It's no longer politically correct I'm told, but Quinn the Inuit would never have caught on. Don't blame me. I waited around a while on the off chance that its handler would turn up, but this didn't happen. The hound then ran off and I assumed knew what it was doing. There were often lots of dogs in the park and owners weren't always immensely vigilant. In any case, I wasn't about to run after a husky. A husky voice would perhaps be a different story.

Striding off, empty of purpose, I stopped briefly to pick up some shit. I should point out that this came from my own small bitch. A pretty little thing, it has the unfortunate habit of walking behind me. This is infuriating since I'm not one for walking backwards unless I really must. The mutt's neck is therefore several inches longer than it should be by virtue of being yanked along; its arse is probably somewhat flatter than it should be for the same reason. Still, we get on all right – most of the time. In any case, if we didn't, she is only a dog and can be put down easily enough. Incidentally, I say and think things that I don't mean. I can't help it and don't know why I do it. I'm fairly sure that gets me off the meat hook.

I actually love dogs. There are only two creatures that remotely deserve to be described as pets, and I've never understood why anyone would have a cat. Cats are just shit dogs. The defence of 'Oh, but they're so much easier' is surely irrelevant. Goldfish are also easier, but I wouldn't have one of those for a pet either. Because they're not. If that is what you call heavy petting, then I pity your girlfriend. I pity her anyway. I've a soft spot for tortoises, particularly the ones who make a bolt for freedom before returning months later, older and wiser. But rodents? Reptiles? Please.

Suddenly, a stooped person of arcane age came upon me, clutching a bag of duck bread. At least, if it wasn't duck bread it was a sorry excuse for a packed lunch – hardly enough to keep even the shallowest furrow ploughman alive. Her furrow, I imagine, would be very shallow. Duck Bread asked me if I enjoyed my new house, didn't listen to the answer, and told me about hers. I might as well have said, "No, it turned out to be a charnel house built over a plague site, you shrivelled old prune," for all the difference it made. I don't know how she knew I'd recently moved to the area, but somehow some people are interested in that kind of thing. She had got as far as describing her fourth previous address when I vainly interjected.

"Oh yes, I know that quite well, my brother has just finished training as a teacher there."

Unfortunately, this formed another segue. Her husband had always wanted to be a teacher apparently. He would have been good at it because he got on with people; he liked them and could always see the good in everyone. The complete opposite of me really, who can always see the bad. Yes, he would have been a good teacher. He always regretted not becoming one. So why the fuck didn't he? I wondered. No reason was given and none was sought.

At this stage, I risked being devoured by my own boredom and so was trying to walk more quickly, with a polite smile on my face. Unfortunately, this prehistoric goat found a new spring in her step and accosted me further. It was as if she'd never met a human being before. Perhaps she was lonely, I don't know. But if people are lonely, they should look lonely, not wear an expression of such irritating beatitude that they wouldn't look out of place in a nunnery. I'm sympathetic, sort of, but some people are just dull. She was.

The odd thing was that despite obviously being a dog walker she had no dog. Women of a certain age, so I am told, would not dream of going for a walk on their own without one. Or least without some excuse for the walk. They can't just go on their own. Men can because they are men. This doesn't quite ring true and mostly seems an excuse for not going out on your own, which applies equally to both genders. Generalisations aside, she was clearly a dog walker since she had a certain gait and was so familiar with mine. We single, pet-owning merchants of misery, who project our emotional needs onto dumb animals rather than be troubled with relationships, can tell such things.

"He's a pretty boy, isn't he?" she remarked rhetorically.

"No, it's a bitch."

"Yes, he's a lovely little chap."

"No, it's a girl – called Bingo."

"Look at his little tail wagging!"

"It's a fucking bitch, you bitch! Leave her alone!"

I wouldn't say that of course but secretly hoped that Bingo tore a piece out of her dewlaps.

By the way, she was called Bingo because I hate campfire songs. As I child I had occasionally suffered the indignity of group activity and was briefly in the Scouts. Managing to duck and weave among the paedophiles, who we are nonsensically terrified into believing run all youth groups, churches and TV shows, I'd learned how to build an A-frame and start a fire using, er... matches. I got so sick of building A-frames that I gave up. I couldn't see what they'd be used for in daily life. Lifting things perhaps? Why not just leave them where they are?

Aside from building A-frames, we had to sing campfire songs occasionally, like the finger-snapping *Ging Gang Goolie*. Inane poppycock. I hated it. *Bingo* was a slightly more erudite campfire song about the eponymous dog. It went something like this:

'There was a man who had a dog,
Bingo was his name.
(So far, so good.)

There was a man who had a dog,
Bingo was his name,
(I know, I heard you the first time.)
B-i-n-g-o, B-i-n-g-o, B-i-n-g-o,
Bingo was his name'.
(Anger rising.)

Back to the first line and repeat ad nauseam, but when you got to the B-i-n-g-o part again, you replaced a letter with a clap. B-i-n-g-clap and so on. Eventually, you got to B-clap-clap-clap-clap. I hated this so much, I find it impossible to put into words.

Most people, I'm sure, would have gone along with it without feeling the need to criticise. But I've always found enforced bonhomie insufferable. I'd called my dog Bingo in an attempt to both rejoin humanity and undermine the patriarchy. Bingo was *her* name. I thought it might make me more congenial towards to my fellow man. Didn't work. I'd thought the same about buying a season ticket to watch Porridge City a few years back, which if anything had the opposite effect. There's nothing more likely to give me a warm feeling than standing amidst a wintery crowd of wankers watching a nil–nil draw.

In any case, that is how she got her name. What is in a name? Nothing except coincidence and history. But since that is all there is, we must make the most of it.

"You've not seen mine, have you?"

"Your what?" I could imagine nothing of hers that I would ever have wanted to see.

"My dog. A big white one."

There was no way she could have owned the husky. It would be like a fly owning a dragon.

"I'm looking after it for a friend," she added.

Some friend! Some looking after. Might as well give an arsonist, or a scout, a box of matches to look after.

"It was running around just now, yes. Really ought to be on a lead." Sound advice.

"I know, yes, but it keeps pulling too hard."

I was speechless.

The duck pond is a short walk across the park and there seemed to be no way to rid myself of this unwanted vestigial twin, this lamprey of tedium. So, I gamely hauled my dog along as she wittered on. There was a commotion ahead. I glanced up, and in the near distance saw a fat figure waddle into view. She looked like a mallard. Mallard was preceded by a delectable young woman who fell more into the swan category. Clearly no relation, she was dressed in a fiery white outfit, which contrasted starkly with her striking mane of black curls. I would have noticed her anyway, I'm sure, but my attention was all the more arrested because she was running purposefully towards a hysterical-sounding woman, who was frantically waving her arms and clawing the air. She appeared to be covered in guts.

"Help! There's been an accident! I think she's dead!" shouted Guts.

I arrived at the duck pond and was very glad I wasn't in charge. A car had slammed on its brakes to avoid hitting the large white dog which had suddenly run out of some bushes. A second car, driving far too close, had ploughed into the back of it. So far, so crumpled, but fairly standard and easy to establish blame: go into someone from behind, whatever the reason, and it's your fault. Insurers get a hard time, but *you* try sorting out a complex claim when no one admits liability. Keep your distance.

This one wouldn't have been complicated, but a third car had apparently careered down the road, which ran alongside the park, and swerved to kill a rabbit. Yes, to kill it rather than avoid it. That there were such people in the world was hard to believe. It's basically why I end up hating everyone. Saves time.

The rabbit's insides had been sprayed over the hysterical woman. The animals at the wheel had driven off, laughing. They might later claim that they were trying to avoid the initial collision, but they were lying. Much less easy to establish blame. If anyone had been injured this would take months, maybe years to sort out. They had presumably not noticed that their own vile idiocy had caused a fourth vehicle to swerve out of the way and hit a cyclist. Mayhem and carnage. One moment, nothing is happening, in the next, life gets plunged into forever changed chaos. Good luck picking the bones out of that.

A yellow bike lay on the bank. Its wheel was still spinning, unlike the world which had stopped for a time, at least for the those at the scene. The cyclist was a young girl, who now lay face down in the pond.

2

Guts, who thought her daughter had just been killed, was not doing well. Mallard was standing there trying to lay an egg. Duck Bread, the annoying neighbour, had disappeared. I hoped that she'd been eaten by the husky.

I was helpless, a useless turd. I'd done a first aid course at work years ago but given it up in case I ever had to do anything. A last aid course might have suited me better – first aid for people who don't like blood or things that are broken. Fortunately, the cavalry had arrived.

"Let me through please, I'm a doctor."

The doctor was something else. She was literally breathtaking. After briefly checking for any obvious dangers in the vicinity, she knelt by the young girl. She rolled her into recovery and got to work: Heimlich manoeuvre to remove water before giving two breaths and starting compressions. I'd read somewhere that the Heimlich manoeuvre wasn't meant to be called that any more for legal reasons. I wasn't sure why you'd need to rename a well-known procedure that had saved countless lives.

100 compressions a minute is hard to sustain, but the good doctor was doing fine. I offered to help and was ignored. Guts was screaming. I'd have been screaming too if I was her.

Dr Castro was on her lunch break. On the rare occasions she managed to have one, she usually went for a run in the research park next door. She didn't usually run into a car crash. Quinn thought that running was for fools. Why run when you can walk? It was one of very many reasons he wasn't a doctor. Being crap at biology was another.

A surname like Castro obviously comes with connotations, which she embraced. As soon as her shift finished, she'd slip into something more comfortable, like combat fatigues, and start chomping fat cigars. 'Soon' was hardly the appropriate word since her shifts lasted 12 hours, if she was lucky. Her father had wanted to call her Fidelia but thankfully commonsense in the form of her mother prevailed. Some people found it necessary to comment on her name.

"Oh, you mean like in Cuba?"

Depending on whether she was interested in talking to them or not she either killed them with a smile, or said "Yes, I have an uncle in Havana." If she was uninterested but obliged to say something, she said "No, Che was the doctor. Fidel was a lawyer."

Mercifully, the young girl eventually choked back into life. If you are going to be knocked headfirst into a duck pond, then do it in a hospital research park. It was one of Porridge City's proudest boasts; internationally renowned for something to do with potatoes and something else to do with the environment. I could never remember which was which.

"You'll be fine, don't worry. There's been an accident, but you'll be OK now."

Guts hugged her daughter. The doctor let her, there were no broken bones. It had been a fairly soft, if abrupt, landing.

"That was amazing, thank God you were here."

Things weren't looking quite so cheery for the driver of the first car, who had still not emerged and who looked twisted. *'Let's twist again, like we did last summer'*. He was face down in the airbag, as if munching a tub of giant marshmallows. His car, and the car that had rear-ended him, now looked like a concertina. Cars are designed to crumple, of course, and that soaks up some of the impact. But this squeezebox wouldn't be playing tunes for a while. Not that squeezeboxes ever do – twiddle dee dee tonic, twiddle dee dee fifth, twiddle dee dee deeeeaarrrgggh! Make it stop. (It seems as though my dislike for inane music has stuck with me since childhood, a sanctuary of resentment.)

I read her name badge, trying not to seem like I was looking at her left breast. Dr Castro was divine. I'd never seen anyone as beautiful or accomplished in my life. I didn't feel worthy of standing there; I thought maybe I'd hurl myself under a tractor. Classic move from an attention-seeking prick. I pointed at her breast instead.

"Oh really, like in Cuba?"

Castro looked at me as if I was an insect. I was. Kafka had nothing on me. I'd have happily turned into a flea if only I was allowed to live on her. I wouldn't bite or anything, just hop about gleefully.

"No, Che was the doctor. Fidel was a lawyer."

She proceeded towards the wreckage.

34

3

A few evenings later, Quinn was sitting in The Rider Haggard pub, waiting for an old schoolfriend called Parker. No doubt the Victorian fabulist writer, bored lawyer, grammar-school-educated traveller would have been thrilled. It was an absurd name, but the chain who owned the venue thought that a bit of literary flair might go down well. Haggard was fairly local, although anyone who had spent at least five minutes in the town could happily be named and laid claim to. He'd owned various properties in his day and was a relatively well-off character in later life, not least because he took a percentage rather than a flat fee for his most famous work. *King Solomon's Mines* was apparently written for a bet, which you could say paid off pretty well and arguably spawned many other novels of a similar ilk. Who knows? Looking backwards is always a lot easier than looking forwards – a lot more data to work with. As far as Quinn knew, he'd never owned a pub.

Quinn spent a lot of time in several of the city pubs; it was part of his unofficial job. Nobody noticed a nonentity. On the night of the accident there had been a group of youths in the corner whom he had immediately despised. Quinn always hated people that he didn't know and went from there. It's a good working hypothesis. 'There's an excellent chance I'm going to hate you once I get to know you, so let's cut to the chase.' There was always a vanishing possibility he might miss out, of course, but on what exactly? Yet another worthless acquaintance, someone else who couldn't save him from the darkness of all-pervading disappointment.

He surely had good reason to despise this bunch, though. In no particular order, they were loud, coarse, ignorant and cocky; young men swimming in their meathead cocktail. He felt humiliated to be near them; not part of their world and yet infected by it. He was a frustrated, small man. He should be in charge!

He often wished he was more given to violence. If he'd had a flamethrower, balls, and immunity from prosecution, then things would be very different round here. He'd have to learn to use the flamethrower first, of course. Not pointing it at his balls for starters. Otherwise, Dr Castro might have a whole new etymology for her surname to conjure with.

Meathead Cocktail had been talking about their latest exploits, to which Quinn paid particular attention:

"Fuck me, yeah, that was mad," said Loud. "Cocky and me were hammering along the Porridge Road when we got to that roundabout near the park, you know. We'd been chasing some wanker all the way from Crappon, right up his arse. He was getting the right hump."

"Right," grunted Ignorant.

"Geezer should have been paying attention to the road not us. He piled right into the back of someone. Twat. I can't be arsed getting involved in someone else's problems, so I wasn't going to hang about. But some old bitch looked across at us like she'd just shat herself. I hate that. Mind your own fucking business. I'll drive how I like, d'ya know wattamean?"

Why they were talking like people from Essex wasn't clear.

"We was laying on the horn, giving her the finger, when this fucking rabbit runs out and we're like, have it!" guffawed Cocky.

"Ride a hag hard, right?" Loud was bellowing with laughter, reliving his best life.

"Hurr hurr hurr," added Coarse. "Nice one."

"All over her fucking front, loving it. Literally perfect timing. Beautiful."

"We pissed right off out of there, no use getting caught up."

"Too right," added Ignorant.

Too wrong. Scum.

There are certain types of young men that the world would be best off without. They won't grow out of it; they will just grow further into it. Quinn had listened with fury. Fury, but not despair. This was one for Parker, his friend. He hadn't referred anyone for a long time and so he was due. Snitches didn't get stitches, snitches got riches. The anonymous ones did at least.

4

Parker arrived as punctually as usual.

"Hi, Quinn, how are things?"

"Oh, fairly slow – until the other day," Quinn replied glumly.

"Cheer up, you miserable bastard."

"Sorry, you must have caught me between smiles."

Parker had spent many years working for Onion Insurance in the city before going freelance. He knew an awful lot about insurance. His favourite job had been working as a loss adjuster. He liked getting to the bottom of things, it gave him a sense of justice. Since going freelance he had retained strong links with his former employer, particularly with the all-seeing analysts, but now had slightly more latitude in how he went about things. He'd adjusted many losses, caused a few as well.

He'd known Quinn since they were kids. Pulled him out of a bog once when he'd sunk in up to his waist trying to prove that it was firm ground. They didn't see much of each other now but met up every few months. Usually when Quinn had something to offer. He liked Quinn well enough, and they went all the way back to primary school shorts, but he did tend towards the negative. An emperor of criticism, a mere plebeian of protest. He was a bit low on action and a bit high on inertia.

Parker was a very different kind of character.

After Quinn had relayed the detail of the incident, he knew that he'd have to pay various calls. Crimes had been committed, but no one had died, and the police had other priorities. That was where he came in. He saw it as his job to investigate crimes of responsibility. Partly because insurance companies paid him to do so. (When it comes to severe road injuries, death is often a lot cheaper than long-term care.) But payment aside, he believed it was only right that you pin blame where you could. Impale it if necessary. The size of the pin was open to negotiation.

People needed to face up to their responsibilities. Parker would be ensuring that Meathead Cocktail did that. He was quite certain this would all be resolved satisfactorily. He was looking forward to it. He'd also speak to the duck-shaped witnesses, the various victims and, of course, to Dr Castro. She had already filled in her report and was clearly unmissable. Like him, she was someone who got on with things.

He might even be able to recruit her.

Slug Life

1 The Plughole

Simeon took a long draught of Rotting Bark's Fungus, his favourite craft ale. There were those who thought this recent fad of taking perfectly good ale and poncing it up with absurd marketing and garish labels was a desecration – he would have none of it. Give the Pale Blues their due, despite some irritating hipster, pseudo anarchic tendencies, they could cough up a decent drop of spit. Who cared if their so-called company values were overblown drivel, a lumpy faced lie to persuade a gormless populace that they treated their production slaves better than most?

His drink accompanied a delicious turd of maggot-meat. Increasingly hard to find these days, he was prepared to pay the necessary premium. He enjoyed the finer things in life and enjoyed demonstrating that he did. Thus, he often spent an evening gorging himself publicly at the new place in town, The Plughole. This latest upmarket gastric pub was, like so many of its contemporaries, an 'improved' version of the previous establishment. For now, it retained a few of its grumbling old regulars, who tended to restrict themselves to the snug bar at the back. Sometimes, they played cabbage, an ancient and noble card game at which fortunes had been won and lost. In time it would be full of Reds and all their self-proclaiming coarseness. Simeon didn't give a crap about that. The old regulars would have to go and be regular somewhere else.

One of them, a Deep Purple called Lime, was slowly making his way towards the back room. An aged rock star, he looked like a tramp but apparently had more money than Bog. A virtuoso harpist in his day, he had led a fairly standard debauched lifestyle until retiring into a relatively civilised form of heavy folk. He was an accomplished representative of his colour. An artist, unlike Simeon, he viewed the Angry Red gastronome with wise contempt and waved only the merest flicker of a feeler in his direction. Lime had seen enough creatures of business in his time and generally viewed them as talentless parasites, who lived on the endeavours of others and created nothing of lasting value. In Simeon's case, that was entirely true.

The Plughole wasn't the quaint old pub it used to be, but times were always changing, before coming back to find themselves again. 'Plus ça change' was one of Lime's favourite quotes from ancient human. Bog knows how many aeons ago some erudite bard had realised the truism. He wasn't against genuine, iconoclastic change: let the Bright and Baby Pinks crash through the detritus that his generation had left and make a better job of it. He didn't mind freshly discovered, uncovered graves at all. But they were rare spasms of light in a dark, festering world. Most innovation was bollocks, an excuse for the noisy to impose themselves on the quiet. As such, he was absolutely and unrelentingly against change for the sake of change, the superficial imposition of something different. Not better, just different. All too often, change was the same as everything staying the same, only more tiring. Some called him cynical, but that was far from the truth. He was just selective. He'd seen it all. He'd seen the worst and the very best of them and he knew he was right.

Another soon to be irregular, an ancient Yellow called Phiz, was slouching in the corner. So-called because he'd suffered a violent salt attack in his youth, he was now quite mad. It would not be long before Phiz embarked on another one of his tales. No one knew whether they were real or myth, or perhaps, as so often, a writhing, entwined combination of the two. Endlessly warring behemoths, devouring both truth and lies then disgorging an excremental belief system between them. His stories were certainly fantastical, but what of that? It was hard to believe any of this could have happened, so why not something else? There was nothing more bizarre, more mundane or more twisted than facts. You simply chose the ones that you believed and fashioned a narrative that best stuck to the wall.

Frock, a Peach-coloured runt, suddenly burst into superficial laughter at some worthless utterance from Simeon. Laughter was too generous a description: it was more of a forced guttural splutter, as if hawking up some phlegm to expectorate into Simeon's pint. That at least would have been a gesture of defiance. The Angry Reds were often accompanied by fawning, snivelling, weaker versions of themselves – the butlers to their hubris. Frock was typical of this nonentity class, largely made up of populist morons with apparently no ability to think for themselves; posturing simpletons, directing their casual, inconspicuous violence towards easy targets.

As Panch, another member of our short cast, shuffled into The Plughole, Frock moved to block his way. Panch was a Teal, the generally most sensitive shade of Blue strata. He was kind; he was something of a poet, something not. We're all poets if we say we are, of course, but you're not a professional until you can live from your art. Panch couldn't, but then hadn't really tried, beyond sharing fragments of his work with close friends. He'd occasionally contemplated showing some of his lyrics to Lime but lacked the confidence. Confidence covers many cracks.

There was no way that he could climb the vast hill of embarrassment about his own work, to stand naked before a listless crowd.

He generally didn't come into the hostelry much. He didn't like the loud, low buffoons who mingled there, seemingly more often of late. He lacked the bonhomie to handle himself in strange company and his shyness appeared aloof. His nervous manner and a dragging limp also tended to make him a target for mockery.

"What's the password?" drawled Frock.

Panch had no reply and ignored the illiterate remark, with a quiver of resentful fear causing an involuntary ripple down his smooth hide. This brought another snigger from his assailant.

"Imp," he muttered, snorting, before turning back to his gross partner. (Imp is among the most offensive terms of abuse in common parlance. As with much slug cant, it is almost impossible to translate because of grotesque nuance and idiom. It impugns virility, ancestry, upbringing and class. A rough translation would be seedless, abandoned, beggaring bastard.)

In such displays of confrontational contempt, Frock thought he had achieved something, marked out his dominance. It was as if he and his cronies were part of some boorish elite, a bullying cadre of the like-minded mindless. This incident was a small thing, an almost irrelevant example of daily aggression. And yet, was it? At what point did an oppressor became a tyrant? Panch had suffered varying degrees of hostility his whole life, he wasn't sure why. Whereas the likes of Frock, and most other Reds, seemed to brush off mild infractions and blunder onwards, these tiny incidents haunted him. They returned, endlessly, marring his peace. He wished he had the strength to take them on, to confront and confound, but he did not. He just wanted to be left alone.

Mutford, the head brewer of Rotting Bark, glanced over to Lime. Both had witnessed the minute scene. Both knew what was necessary. A threshold had been passed and, from that innocuous moment, the future became irrevocable.

2 Etymology – A Spasmodic Interlude

The Slugs exist in a distant, post-human community, the terminology of which requires some brief explanation. They have evolved over countless aeons from their horror-inducing, prehistoric ancestors. Slug society is broadly split into two strata called Blues and Reds. They are generally identifiable, and even defined by their colour, into roles and prejudices, although there is some overlap. Each strata is split into three main types:

Blues – generally anti-establishment, leftish, artists
Deep Purple – rocker types, such as Lime
Pale Blues – faux cool, 'alternative' liberals, such as Mutford from the Rotting Bark Brewery
Teal – gentle, lazy, slightly ineffectual dreamer sorts, like Panch

Reds – generally establishment, rightish, not artists
Angry Reds –bullying, selfish bastards, often vulgarians or plain ignorant, such as Simeon. (Think of your worst ever boss and you might be close.)
Peach – essentially these are weaker, servile versions of Angry Reds, for instance Frock

Orange – more apathetic than actively hostile, broadly toe the line

Outside the two main strata are the Yellows – tellers of tales, perhaps riven by madness, like Phiz. It is not always clear whether they are insane or wise. Perhaps too much knowledge has devoured their minds.

Pinks – these are the youth, the new spawn with colours as yet undetermined
Bright pinks – young adults, some delinquency
Baby Pinks – children

That aside, there are a few other forces that need to be defined. Slug society is governed by the Slaw. We can think of these as both police and judiciary. They tend to be Reds. Partly as a result of the overriding influence and power of the Slaw, other syndicates have emerged. One of the most notable of these is the so-called Steam. This is a secretive, interventionist organisation – a kind of nonprofit Mafia. Its structures and protocols are opaque, naturally, and cannot be succinctly discussed here. One of the principal activities of Steam is to act as a moral guardian of decency, in particular dealing with low-level, cumulative crimes that the Slaw will not bother to investigate. They dispense ex-judiciary, frontier justice.

The Steam's reluctant philosophy is that extreme sanction is justified when the State has failed. In some cases, only history could separate terrorist from freedom fighter and the removal of malignant individuals, unpunished by the law, is acceptable. However, they generally operate a policy of low-profile intervention. At the more prosaic level, they believe that selfishness is a crime and that narcissists and bullies will dominate unless they are ruthlessly undermined. They predict a world full of Angry Reds and Peaches and abhor that vision.

Once a slug is determined to be unacceptably pernicious to others, they can be dealt with using an execution procedure known as Double Rending. The determination can take some time, or it can be manifest from the moment a Pink reaches adulthood. Various warnings may take place before a Double Rending verdict is pronounced. Once pronounced, the verdict is almost never commuted.

The obvious question, of course, is why then doesn't everyone behave well? Why indeed! The Steam isn't everywhere; it is a clandestine, illegal organisation that is therefore obliged to maintain a limited profile. It is not a state operator, and the State, seemingly, chooses to tolerate bad behaviour. As with most crime, it is not punishment that concerns perpetrators as much as the fear of being caught. Slugs are prone to disappearance and death – that in itself is no great matter for comment. The Steam, therefore, is sometimes viewed as apocryphal until it is too late. But the main reason that the presence of the Steam doesn't lead to benign, universally good neighbours is that some slugs are just arrogant and vile. They cannot help themselves. Or rather, they choose not to.

It should also be noted that slugs are hermaphrodite and there is no such thing as gender. Their mating rituals are revolting to say the least and are largely unchanged from the most primal mythological times. Upon arousal and excited nibbling, two consensual adults will form a kind of squirming heart shape. If the couple are particularly flamboyant, they might hang from a thick line of excreted slime. Large, phallic organs protrude from the backs of both their heads and are inserted into the recipient. This two-way coupling can last for hours. Afterwards, these vast members are corkscrewed back into their owners' bodies but can get stuck. If that happens the receiving slug simply chews off the offending article before bidding their mate goodnight. That's evolution for you. Size is not everything in the slug world.

One final point: given the sometimes barbaric nature of their behaviour, it is fortunate that slugs don't feel pain. At least, we don't think they do.

3 Phiz Talks

"There were giants, once. They left no bones."

Phiz was particularly incoherent this evening, either mumbling insensate drivel or somehow recalling mystical genetic memories from a collective well of shared endless time. Who knew. Most assumed the first. Among other themes, death featured prominently. It always seemed to. After five pints of Fungus, conversation tended to be maudlin. Monologues even more so.

"No one knows how, or why, the giants disappeared, but they were gone, in the twitching of a feeler. In geological terms, an instantaneous cataclysm; extirpated without a trace. They were cruel to us and to themselves. Carnage followed in their wake. Ancient brothers, wrapped in shrouds of white and crushed beneath a mighty force. Trapped in a suffocating bag of rocks, slowly dissolving life away; held up briefly to the light and then dropped into a wet hole, before a storm-like bellow of disgust. A curse on all slugs!"

He swivelled an eye stalk towards his mantle briefly, as if looking around. But it was just an involuntary twitch; he saw nothing. He was unaware of the slight communication around him, of hidden plans afoot.

"A huge, black slug king, the like of which has never since been seen, ruled a forest enclave in the East. Hurled into the trees by an unseen hand, as jest. For fun! He sailed through blue skies in this verdant glade, briefly flying. Briefly leaving this earth, then impaled on a branch and hung, dripping. No sacrifice, no appeasement. A simple killing. His revenge would echo through time, an endless quiver of revulsion passed on through generations of fear."

"We have endured, though, we survived. They would never be rid of us – now we are rid of them. Patience. Crawl, eat, sleep. Lead a virtuous life! We are all slugs, but not all of us are slime."

And so on and so forth. Ramblings. Phiz had lost his life partner years ago and had never been the same since. Not all couples stayed together for life, but some did. Love among slugs was a precious thing: once lost, never recovered. He stopped, trembling, lost in memories.

"I'll never know another like them. Three Baby Pinks, we had. They saw past this," he murmured, gesturing to his scars. He had a portrait of his family on the mantelpiece at home. In it, his youngest child gazed up at him with love, unaware of the pain that life could suddenly bring, blind to any disfigurement.

"That's very true, Phiz," patronised Simeon, his flesh rolls quivering with a fake chuckle. *For Bog's sake, why won't the ugly old bastard zip it?* he thought, rolling his eye stalks at Frock.

"Jonas Crust, doesn't he ever shut the funt up?" agreed the latter.

4 Vanishing

Necessary time passed, consultations held, verdict announced, and arrangements made. It had been a while coming and so the final process was a slick one, a triumph of light-touch bureaucracy. There was no right of appeal: by this stage the accused and the guilty were one and the same. Unamended ways could only be tolerated for so long.

Tonight, Frock would die. The details are available elsewhere but, in essence, he was a malignant individual whose death would be better for everyone who suffered his drip-fed poison. Numerous times he had been referred to the Slaw; numerous times they had failed to act. Insufficient evidence, insufficient resources, insufficient crimes. No one cared that he ruined lives, used his connections with various Angry Reds to avail himself a swaggering brutality. He picked on the weak, he was selfish, and there were no legitimate means to deal with him. Bog was long since dead and in a Bogless world there could be no divine justice to redeem the iniquities of life. No one cared about his low-level abuses of civility, his vicious, ignorant spite. No one cared that he contaminated those around him with piggy, self-absorbed greed.

But there were those who *did* care. The unnamed, the self-appointed guardians of decency. Were they any better than the thugs they condemned? Yes, I believe they were.

Soon after he emerged from The Plughole and began slithering home, Frock became aware of a dank, slow movement in the darkness. A drawing of shadows. He hastened, somewhat.

There was a limit to how fast his belly could be hauled. The others, somehow, could move more quickly. Escape was not generally an option for slugs.

"It was one too many this evening, dung piece," razored a sibilant voice, suddenly beside him. "I am a representative of the Steam." One spoke while another, darker still, remained silent.

Slugs could not, as far as we know, feel pain. But they could feel terror.

"You have ignored our warnings, our gestures, and your behaviour has continued unabated. You are deemed malignant, a tumour. There is no redemption."

Frock had heard of such things, had dismissed them as childhood nightmares. Of course he had. How could anyone remain sane otherwise? His minor misdemeanours were surely no cause for complaint. Surely, they could talk about this!

They could not.

"But..." Frock began.

The creature beside him sighed. His accomplice shuffled impatiently. Two silent and twisted horrors who knew their work.

"Be quiet. Things will be worse if you are not quiet."

"How could they be any worse!" Frock mewled.

Nonetheless, after that he took their advice. Speed was of the essence in slug killing. Better to be torn asunder than slowly baked under a grill for hours, after all. Nobody wants to be a biscuit. The details do not matter here. Fair to say that the remains of this intervention would not pass the mantelpiece test for art. Avant-garde is one thing, actual cutting edge is another.

The pile of soft tissue, guts and slime previously known as Frock was lifted into a pickchit. This is a wheelbarrow of sorts, specifically used for transporting dead matter. Buccal mass, radula, stomach and oesophagus slopped across the bottom of this terminal carriage. His internal shell would need a little more attention during the disposal process but was only of modest size. A useful source of vitamins.

*

Mutford waited beside the entrance to the Rotting Bark Brewery, whistling a mournful tune. *Ballad For an Eye Stalk* was perhaps the most enduring example of Lime's artistic output. They went back a long way, had shared some mildly riotous times as Bright Pinks in the first flush of youth. Neither had strayed too far from decency, though; they had heeded warnings and never harmed another. Easy enough, you'd have thought, to be kind. But apparently it was not. Even easier to be cruel.

In time, they had been approached by the Steam and drifted naturally into their current roles within its labyrinthine hierarchy. It wasn't a matter of indoctrination; it was a matter of necessity, as far as he could tell. They were there to makes things better. He believed that things would be much worse without them and there was no profit incentive to distort their ethos. They acted out of charity.

All vigilantes thought they were doing the right thing, of course. Hopefully, some were.

5 Epilogue – A Last Brew

Simeon had been a bit more subdued of late. It could be that he had finally learned chagrin or was suffering from piles. Or perhaps he was just considering his options. A week after the disappearance of Frock, he had received a letter to his business address at The Log retail park. It was marked with the rare, renowned sickle seal. Upon timorous opening, it revealed just one sentence and an edict:

The eyes of the Steam are on you. Do not speak of this.

Icy fear had sprawled across his guts. It was soon grappled by his overbearing arrogance and air of invulnerability. "Do-gooder pricks," he fumed. "Who the funt did they think they were, telling *him* how to behave decently? Funting parent funters." His vocabulary was even more lamentable than usual when enraged or scared. He did not scare well.

Now, in The Plughole a few nights later, he continued to ponder. Something needed to be done.

*

Panch was not sad to hear of Frock's presumed demise. It seemed to be a case of one tormentor down, none to go. The vanishing of the bully had generated a ripple effect. For a time, at least, his unassuming life had found peace. The black stone of oppression was rolled aside, and freedom peered both ways.

He had finally found the courage to talk to Lime, who he'd actually found to be an approachable sort, albeit somewhat gruff and abrupt. Talking to this particular hero was not a disappointment. Panch had even mentioned his lyrics, which had been met with polite interest. He guessed that aged rock stars got bored with starlets.

Lime gestured him over again this evening. "Those words you mentioned, maybe I can take a look."

Panch beamed from feeler to feeler.

*

Simeon took a long draught of Rotting Bark's newest offering, Payback Porter. A pitch-black, foamy brew with toadstool notes and an almost deceased, fleshy finish.

El Camino

1

The place hadn't even heard about better times. A room that would have been closed for repairs in Hell was all they had to offer. He took it. A flat excuse for dead beer was all they had to drink. It was warmer than the sun and tasted like a mouse had been breeding in the barrel. But better than nothing. His feet felt like someone was trying to squeeze juice out of them and his backside felt like he'd been dangling it in margarine. It had been a long, hot day and he was still unsettled after what had occurred. All he wanted was to take the weight off in the shade. This poor excuse for a dwelling certainly had plenty of that.

Weary travellers walking on bloody stumps for feet, who hadn't eaten for a week, would arrive, and say, "Screw this, man, let's press on." Dogs wouldn't even pause to piss on the front step. He half expected to see a nativity start up before long. But he wasn't fussy. Tonight, he could sleep anywhere.

In the corner a man was growing a beard. It was coming on well but the bald patch on his right cheek would remain, like a miniature monk's head drowning in a donkey's backside. Something like that, anyway. The waitress, who had a beard of her own, brought him over a snack which looked as though it might have been treating a blister for three days. He'd never seen grey food before. He'd rather have snacked on his own balls. A fly landed on it before leaving in disgust.

He decided to try to freshen up slightly. He could have achieved this by diving into a pile of manure but there wasn't one to hand, so he went to look for the facilities. Going down to the toilet was like a return trip up a bowel. Afterwards, he tried to maintain some vestige of dignity by washing his hands. Naturally the tap exploded liquid, which might have been water once, back all over his shirt and crotch. He returned to the bar looking like he'd pissed himself twice. An oafish humanoid in a green shirt was shouting something about rice. Nobody paid him any attention.

A tall, bald shit that nobody knew walked in, saying "Hola!" to everyone, as though he'd never been away. He was wearing knee-length socks and sandals, for God's sake. Socks and sandals! Even the barmaid had more sartorial elegance and she appeared to be wearing a sleeping bag with holes torn out of the bottom. Maybe the last man she'd had in there had chewed his way out in an attempt to escape.

He was on a pilgrimage, or so he'd been told. He was mainly on a long walk. Going on foot to Santiago, which, until yesterday, he'd not realised meant Saint James. He'd known that in the cathedral there was a silver casket containing Saint James's bones, or at least a relic purporting to be them, but he'd not twigged that Iago was simply James in Spanish. For obvious reasons, he'd always associated the name Iago with devious malice – he wasn't sure that Jimmy would have had the same devastating influence in *Othello*. Presumably the Bard was familiar with the ludicrous, centuries too late, Moor slaying myths about Saint James, so it all made sense.

There had only been time to complete the last 100 miles or so of this old pilgrim route, which had originally started in Paris during the Middle Ages. Back then, it would have been an epic endeavour, pursued by people who genuinely believed it was a route to salvation. Now, it mainly seemed to be an excuse for young people to wander around getting laid. Not that there was anything wrong in that. He wasn't averse to enlightenment and even had vague traces of residual religion. He and God had an understanding. But the most spiritual moment so far had been the discovery of an excellent sherry cask cognac, which sadly wasn't available in this establishment.

Walking had always been his preferred form of exercise, and it had been a decent saunter so far, with history awash on either side. As usual on such foreign excursions it was the grisly details that struck him most profoundly. He'd seen a church fresco earlier of someone who looked like he was about to play the saw in a kind of 15th-century monastic hoedown band. But the long-legged guide had advised him that saints were often depicted holding the means of their unspeakable demise. He'd come across a statue of the same martyr in the town square, killed by a saw for his faith. As well as being impressed with such devotion, he found it insane. He was fairly sure he'd deny any faith he had in that situation. The sun goes around the earth? Fine with me. The moon is made of cheese? Whatever you say.

Being killed by a saw is bad enough, you might think, but this was a particularly repulsive variation. Evidently this favoured form of execution involved being sawn in half upwards from the groin. Or downwards if you were tied by the ankles to a beam, which was easier for the executioners. Nice guys the Romans: feed people to lions, nail them to crosses, stone them, boil them. Christ, people must have been bored in the days before television.

How could such things even be possible? Surely it was a gross exaggeration made up by the church to extol the piety of its heroes. Apparently not.

In Florence he'd seen a horrific picture of Saint Lawrence being roasted. Lawrence looked fairly sanguine about the whole thing. He failed to understand but was intrigued by the bizarre, essentially Catholic, traits of piety, dogma, guilt and beatification of heroic agony, as if revelling in misery. It was like some kind of perverse fairy tale. Saint Bartholomew was flayed alive! He recalled the famous image of him holding his skin in the Judgement Day portion of the Sistine Chapel ceiling. His knowledge of art was minimal and mainly gruesome.

What kind of a person could do these things to another human being? Actually, maybe *he* could if the gorilla in green didn't stop shouting about rice. Life might have been cheaper in the good old days, but surely it was worth more than being sawn in half upwards from the balls. He crossed his legs.

Most of the journey had been sparsely, but regularly, populated with fellow travellers. Mainly people walking, but with the occasional cyclist. Sometimes pushing, sometimes carrying their bike like a wheeled cross, but generally scything up behind him then rushing past. What the fuck is wrong with a bell? he'd wondered. These idiots weren't on any kind of spiritual expedition, they were just poseurs, riding around in skintight suits with their bloody helmets and shades. Pricks. Mainly people walking, though.

Some walked in groups, others started conversations with strangers. He tended to walk selfishly, at his own pace. He'd once gone on a walking holiday with a doomed companion and had marched off up a snow-covered hill. She'd somehow managed to plunge one leg into a hole and been helped out of it by a passing do-gooder. When he eventually waited for her to catch up, she had complained, "It was lucky that man helped me up."

He'd replied, "Yes, it was," before marching off again. Now he tended to walk alone.

2

Earlier in the day, a couple of miles from town, he'd decided to go slightly off track to find an ancient chapel. There were plenty around. He'd been unable to sleep during a grim night in a hostel the previous evening and had set off before light. So, time was on his side as he approached the stage end. Plenty of daylight left to tick off another charming village and clock up another couple of miles. Time had other ideas.

There was no way he was staying in a hostel again. He was too old to be sharing a box-sized dormitory with 16 people. There weren't 16 people he wanted to share the world with, let alone a box. Fair to say he wasn't finding companionship and brotherly love crucial aspects of this experience. Didn't matter how bad the place was tonight he was sleeping alone. Unless of course he fell into the arms of some shady señorita, which seemed about as likely as him dying for his faith.

As he entered the village and approached the chapel, he was immediately aware of a change in tone – in *presence*. There were no friendly faces offering sustenance at a fair price, no immediate evidence of any activity at all. A few decrepit farmhouses, long since abandoned for better lives, a few old pieces of machinery lying around. There had been similar shuttered farms along the way, presumably no longer viable as history caught up and devoured them. But these seemed haggard, somehow, jaded, as if offended by their dereliction. There were also inhabited houses off to one side of the street, but these were quiet and lacking in substance. Marauding weeds formed most of the vegetation, an occasional splash of sun-bleached paint the only colour. Nothing much here was touched by human hand.

He heard someone moving around inside one of the barns. An odd-looking fellow with shaggy eyes emerged after a few moments. He was dragging a sack. It was clear that the sack might just as easily have contained body parts as wood. Unfortunately for him, the odd fellow looked up and caught him staring. Normally he would return a stare, a belligerence that had probably grown out of childhood thugs asking, "What are you looking at?" He resented being asked. He resented the threat of violence; he resented his own impotence in the face of it.

But on this occasion, he wished he could look away. The odd fellow was way more than odd. The face of this creature, for it could scarcely be human, was the most terrifying thing he had ever seen. A mask of horror without the mask, it exuded evil. The thing had stopped moving, that would have been unbearable. It stared back at him with greedy hatred. It had the eyes of a devil. Maybe *the* devil.

Although it looked, more or less, *Homo sapiens*, there was something cavernous about its closed mouth. A mouth that could swallow worlds. Its snout was smeared sideways as if daubed on as an afterthought; hair sprouted from what passed as ears and was knotted into vast sideburns. These undesirable features were nothing, though, compared to its eyes. Compared to its eyes, the other features could have been copied directly from a face cream advert.

Its eyes were stagnant. They rotted. Pus green with red clots – try this delicious new flavour of Yo, Gut! The exciting new brand of self-actualising congealed milk, made by philosophers for philosophers. Curds and why. These were eyes that could have gazed upon any horror and remained unblinking. They had.

Almost literally he tore himself away. It felt like he had left a chunk of himself stuck to the road, his guts tugging, hooked on a branch. Perhaps this thing would come and collect it later, a local flesh tax. Add it to its goody bag for the worst children's party ever. It would have made a bad clown.

He walked on, praying that he wouldn't be followed. There was no way he was looking back! Why the fuck would Lot's wife have looked back? Just one more glance at my good old happy home on the range. Don't worry kids, we'll be back one day. Sodom wasn't exactly *The Little House on the Prairie*. No, he wasn't going to be looking back. He didn't even want to be hearing back. If he was being followed, he would die. Even if an owl god had appeared and twisted his head round 180 degrees, he'd have walked backwards in spite.

Here's a thing: owls don't have eyeballs! Their eyes are fixed in place, which is why they have to twist their heads round to see anything. Strange design. He didn't need any eyeballs either at the moment. On reflection, he had decided that staying on track was a considerably better idea.

Looking straight ahead, he took very long strides.

3

After eschewing the blister meal, he'd decided to attempt the wine. The barmaid had shambled off to get some a while ago, presumably from a crate in the cellar. After all, the wine couldn't be any worse than the beer. Even if the cocooned barmaid had made it out of her own menstrual flow, collected for years and fermented in a chemical toilet, it would have been an improvement on that odiferous effluent.

It was actually pretty good! In fact, it was amazing. It tasted more like port than wine. Very posh. Too bad he hadn't dressed for dinner. Thank you, my good man, just pass this on to the left. He'd have to get his calories from drink this evening, bulked up by the impeccable dry sausage he kept in his rucksack for emergencies. The cheese had unfortunately gone. He was living proof that you could live on cheese, sausage and wine. For how long, who knew. The velvety nectar soon eased him into a comfortable fug. He'd all but forgotten about his earlier encounter.

*

He woke up frozen. It had happened before. The condition is called sleep paralysis and it's fairly common. No less unpleasant for that, of course. Stubbing your toe is fairly common but the annual Belford Toe Stubbing Competition never attracts many entrants. Contestants are blindfolded, spun around and then have to walk very quickly among randomly placed anvils.

During sleep paralysis you're awake but unable to move, speak or open your eyes. It can feel like someone is in your room. That someone might also be pressing down on your chest. The

NHS website says that you may feel frightened! No shit, Sherlock. I can't move or see and I *feel* like there is someone in my room. Sounds relaxing. They might as well say that you may feel a twinge when giving birth, or some mild discomfort while having your stomach pumped; a dull ache if repeatedly punched in the balls.

Apparently not eating a huge meal, not drinking alcohol or coffee and not smoking helped to avoid it. The same things helped to avoid living. You make as well add not shagging to the list. He'd rather have sleep paralysis.

Not that he was able to think so coherently at the moment. A spreading sense of terror enveloped his dislocated state, feeding on his limited consciousness. Just. Wake. Up. He couldn't force himself to. It still felt like a bad dream. The fucking wine. There was no feeling, only an increasingly panicked numbness. His muscles failed to clench as he tried desperately to force them into a response. He could hear a thudding noise outside, a kind of regular beat. Footsteps on the stairs perhaps. But also, an extra, behind-the-beat knocking. A surrogate tempo. Something being dragged up the stairs perhaps.
Just.
Wake.
Up.

There was a creature in the room. It glinted in the moonlight. Not much romance in this moonlight, though; it was more the scooping out of your insides kind of moonlight. Clair de spoon. It didn't move; it just stared with putrid eyes.

Please, let me wake up, I'll do anything if I can just wake up. I'll believe in anything.

It was now crouched over him, backwards and bending, its arm moving with intent in a studied, rhythmic motion. A hideous friction, moist and slithering. The sound of scraping fingernails. Then only blackness.

4

Finally, he woke up. The room felt different, cleaner. He felt safe. Thank Christ. Now he'd believe in anything. His leg seemed twisted, his knee in the wrong place, somehow. Voices now, white coats in the pale room.

"I think he is coming round."

"Looks like it."

"Can you hear us?"

He managed to turn his head towards the soothing sound. The sound of authority. An angel with authority.

"I'm afraid you've been involved in an accident, and we've had to operate, but you're going to be all right. You were found outside in the early hours of the morning – it looks as though you were hit by a vehicle. For now, just rest. We're going to keep you comfortable for a while and then we can talk about the next steps."

It happened all the time: people strayed from the path and got lost. He was lucky that he had been found so quickly otherwise it might have been too late. Although admittedly pretty unlucky to have been in that state in the first place. Maybe whoever hit him had a sudden pang of conscience and called for roadside assistance. Or dropped him off on the way to collect a pizza.

Bewildered, he tried to squirm out a response:

"Nnnn! Thgh nt appnnn. I was unttkd. Maannc szz."

"Well, that's fine, don't worry. We can talk later."

"Nnnn! Ffffsss. Lushztn. Hairy bastard!"

The doctor raised her eyebrows. This could definitely wait until later. She nodded to the nurse who dispensed some more happy juice.

"Just rest for now."

There weren't all that many English-speaking doctors in Spain, let alone in this hospital, and she tended to pick up the Brits if she was on shift. She'd worked in the UK for several years but returned soon after the delightful Brexit vote. She wasn't about to stay in a country that didn't want her. She'd also got fed up with the rain and the moaning, but it was mostly the vote. A desire to stop people 'Coming over here, stealing our men!' was ignorant enough. But wanting them to stop 'Coming over here, healing our sick and injured!' was a bit self-defeating. Create a world-leading state healthcare system and then spend the next 70 years undermining it. Seemed like a strange way to operate.

The referendum itself was a shocker. All referendums are! She was relatively well-educated and didn't have a clue. It seemed to her that there were a minority of people who voted to leave in good conscience, concerned about the erosion of democratic oversight. But the vast majority of people voted for quite different reasons. She knew one person who had ticked leave because 'they don't vote for us in the Eurovision song contest.' Right. Perhaps there were equally inane reasons on the other side.

The obsession with EU rules was just plain bizarre. Why not ignore them like everyone else? Why invent your own versions? According to Charles Dickens, the British literally created bureaucracy, yet now they wanted to reduce red tape. Enjoy all that control you've taken back. It was going to be slicker than a greased weasel now.

Politics was sicker than the man in this bed. She used to be interested but was now convinced that it was mostly just propaganda and corruption. Classic divide and conquer. Those billions siphoned off from public funds – what? Don't look there. Revolving doors? Ludicrous! The parasitic rich? Lovely people! It's the parasitic poor you need to be worried about. Them and the brown ones over there. It's their fault. Depressing, really.

The nurse straightened his cleaner, whiter sheets and closed the door on the way out.

He needed to explain to them what had happened, but no words had emerged. Tell them about the beast from hell with decaying eyes. Surely, they'd understand! He couldn't remember anything after seeing the hunched figure in his bedroom. He wished he couldn't remember that, either.

No idea how he'd arrived. But he felt safe at least. That was good. His knee itched like an ant-filled arse. If only he could scratch it. He tried to reach down. He could just about hear a motorbike firing up outside. His muscles raged, it felt like he was clawing his way out of time. But eventually his hand made it down far enough. Too far.

"Whaaaaa! Hllllp! Arrggnn!!" Before too long, the drugs kicked in.

As they wafted down the corridor, the medical staff exchanged a few more words:

"Poor guy."

"Yes, quite an unusual injury. Taken clean off."

The doctor wondered whether the rest of his leg was now still stuck on the undercarriage, a trophy to carnage. Some pilgrimage that had turned out to be. Perhaps he could still hop to the cathedral and get healed, but it seemed a long shot.

A couple of miles out of town, the sack was now a little heavier.

Re(garding) Maniacs

Cast
Monk – the best player but given to long delays
Frazer – a low-level threat of violence
The Stable – tedious and takes things literally
Doberman – impassive and carefree
Fat Henge – yet to arrive
Dan – not part of the gang
Good guys – real names

Without the long delays and ranting, it was no fun. Unfortunately for everyone else the opposite was true. They gathered, grudgingly, every couple of months or so to have a fairly lousy time. This watery remnant of a once uninterrupted flow, this evaporating puddle of weary slash, was all that remained. Eventually, someone would suggest moving to quarterly, then twice yearly (which Doberman would insist on miscalling biannually) then, in time, they'd wonder why they'd ever bothered at all.

"Can you just play?" said The Stable. Ludicrous nickname, picked up from nowhere and something to do with leaving doors open. Maybe he was the new Messiah. It could also refer to his monotone mental state: lack of disorder disorder (LDD). He, more than most, found Monk's alternate daydreaming and musing intolerable. It would have been interminable as well except that it wasn't. Not yet anyway. That was the thing with eternity, it didn't half drag on. The Stable, if nothing else, was precise. Perhaps pretending to take everything extremely seriously was his way of being frivolous, but it didn't really work. Unless his aim was to come across as a humourless cock, in which case it worked very well.

Monk gazed for a moment before turning his attention briefly to the matter in hand. "What? Whose turn is it?"

"Honestly! Will you just pay some attention, just some, just for one minute." The Stable never swore, nobody knew why. It's not as if he had a prodigious vocabulary or ever read anything except books about physics. He might as well swear.

"It's on you, Monk," said Doberman. This dog-faced, mother-sniffer couldn't even spell his own name correctly.

"What do you mean it's on me? What does that even mean?"

"It's your turn to play, for God's sake. Will you just make an effort. Please, just try to concentrate on the game," said The Stable.

His interventions were about as effective as belching into a hurricane.

"Relax, man. It's not the world championships," said Monk.

"No, but we're here to play."

"You might be, I'm not. Nothing you can ever say will make the slightest difference to me."

That shut The Stable door up for a while.

Doberman laughed. He didn't care; he just found the evenings mildly diverting. He was an impassive fellow.

There was an American in the bar tonight. Maybe that's why it was being called a bar rather than a pub. Wankers. He kept intruding into their conversation, as if they were remotely interested in his opinion about anything; as if his presence was in any way required. Naturally, he had insisted on telling them he was called Dan despite no one giving the slightest shit. They wouldn't have cared if his name was Rumplestiltskin. Dan kept butting into their game with inane remarks, such as, "That's what I'm talking about," or, "You got this." If he had said, "Get in the hole," then Frazer would have ripped his throat out. Frazer was always threatening to rip someone's throat out. He'd been doing so since school and never quite grown out of the habit. Monk had no idea why they endured him.

Dan had the peculiarly American habit of talking excitedly about things that were not remotely exciting. Jutting into everyone else's business as if he had some unstated right to involvement; as if everyone wanted to hear what he had to say. No one did.

"Hell yes!" offered Dan, apropos of nothing.

Being a child of the '70s, Monk had necessarily owned an Action Man. An Action Man *doll* in fact, although they were not generally called dolls. Girls had dolls, amongst other gender appropriate playthings. This crew-cut hunk of muscle could be kitted out in various military garb and employed in a variety of manly pursuits. He had GRIPPING HANDS that could 'hold' guns and the like. He could also GRIP HANDS with other Action Men for no apparent reason. If you and your friends had several dolls, they could be linked together, human chains of macho pointlessness. It had been fun at the time, though, and Monk didn't really buy into the 'violent toys beget violent behaviour' nonsense. It's fairly clear that humans are violent anyway and would be more so if they could get away with it. Humans are inhuman.

As well as the basic Action Man, there was an EAGLE-EYED version whose eyes could be slid right and left with a small lever. This created conflict in play when wholly realistic scenarios were enacted whereby EAGLE-EYED Action Man could see things that the other Action Men could not. No way, man, those pricks could only look straight ahead.

"You can't see that, it's out of your peripheral vision. Only Eagle Eye can."

"I can just turn my head."

"No, you can't, you wouldn't think to. Only Eagle Eye can see the plastic dog creeping up to tear your throat out."

"Not fair! You can't just keep making things up!"

And so on.

Monk and his brothers had also had a TALKING COMMANDER Action Man. This was a superb evolution. By virtue of a pull string in his back, the TALKING COMMANDER could issue orders: "Send out the patrol," "Enemy tanks approaching," "What's the password?" and, quite specifically, "Advance in single file." (There were two others that he couldn't remember.) This created more play opportunities, although since the commands were random, it could get confusing. When TALKING COMMANDER was supposed to be saying, "What's the password?" he might say, "Advance in single file," several times first. No, what's the fucking password, dickhead? There was a reason most children's toys got thrown away. Spare me the sloppy sentimentality – toys get slung because they stink.

TALKING COMMANDER was great though, and a game within a game emerged which was to see how many times he could be made to randomly say the same thing. The 'world' record was saying "Enemy tanks approaching" 13 times. They must be here by now, for fuck's sake! Monk had worked out that this was about a 1 in 2 billion chance, which seemed pretty high. Maybe it wasn't random after all. Perhaps there were micro adjustments made when pulling out the string to make him talk. Or maybe children are prone to exaggeration. Most children, anyway. The Stable had never exaggerated. If asked, he would have said his dick was slightly below average sized.

It struck Monk that Dan was like an *In*action Man; a useless, torpid fat turd, uttering asinine remarks without respite. A man without volition, whose 'gripping hands' could be used to scratch his arse but little else. He wondered who was pulling his strings.

Wool gathering again.

*

7.45pm: start of rant.

"So, it's like this: all you do is type until you get to 3000 words and then stop. Do that 10 times and you've got a short, awful novel. Keep spewing them out until you can spew no more. Don't stop, not even for a second. If you do stop, then just go back and fill in the cracks like a builder on speed, or a teenage male on fantasy. That way, you can produce stream of consciousness nonsense in record time. Just like Americans in

73

the 1950s who discovered James Joyce far too late and then tried to be angry about it. *Catcher in the Rye*? Good grief. It's one of the most overrated books ever written. It had literally nothing to do with John Lennon and would have been forgotten long ago if his sick fuck murderer hadn't been insane. Hard to believe that it was ever shocking in any way. No wonder nobody gives a toss about it now. But then, we weren't there. It's not even possible that people didn't think exactly the same things as Bollinger before he bothered to write some of them down. I don't know why he did bother actually. I mean, really. All you do is talk in this disjointed, illiterate way and say 'goddam phoney' every four bars and we're meant to believe it? Jesus Christ. Talking of bars, I'll give them jazz, the Americans. There, we follow. Okay, so they might not have invented it directly, but they more or less did. We don't have time for a history lesson, for fuck's sake. I'm not sure what else I'd give them, but I'll give them jazz: Louis, Duke, Charlie et al. make up for a multitude of sins. Good job, really.

"Back to shocking (really?) youth American literature: offhand, the only book I can think of that is similar but worse than *Catcher* (first name terms you see) is *On the Road*. Fuck me slowly. If I was on the road with that dickhead, I'd have been rolling down the window and taking my chances. It's the literary equivalent of dysentery. Amoebic at that, the bad kind. (And he should know! See elsewhere – Ed). But then Caramac wasn't a writer, he was a typist, to paraphrase Truman Capote. I'd imagine Truman (still first name) was a bit of a prick in real life. But then all artists are, that's why they have to live outside it. Funny people are pricks in real life too, it goes without saying. (Life is in brackets, or parentheses if you prefer. I don't.) I don't need to quote long words in order to prove how goddam clever I am. Jesus Christ. Are you bored yet? You will be soon!

"Back to Jack, and off we go. The trouble is, in slating Jack I have to acknowledge that Dylan liked him. That really kicks me in the balls because Dylan (not first name terms, that would be like being on first name terms with God) is the man, the main man. The closest thing that rock gets to genius, which is not saying that much because it's such a trite, besmirched word now. Someone can be a legend for sitting by a swimming pool, it's great. I don't know where you go from there, really. Everything Dylan touches turns to gold in my opinion, which is not really true. But if you've not listened to his first seven albums then stop what you're doing immediately and get them out now. If you haven't even bought them, shame on you. Fuck streaming, make an effort, man. I was lying about the first six, it's two to seven. The first album doesn't really count; you can use it as a coaster for the next cup of tea. Or one more cup of coffee, even. It was basically a demo recorded in around five minutes. Much like his other albums, to some extent. Now people take five years to make one and it's generally shit. I'm not sure what happened. There's plenty of great music around still, I just don't know where to find it. I'm not one of these tired bar room bores who prattle that the '60s were the best. Were they fuck! The best of its largely tedious output might have endured, but most stuff hasn't, thank Christ. Stop talking about Bob Dylan! Jesus, as if enough hasn't already been said. The point is that perhaps you need to read Caramac (or Bollinger or whoever) at an impressionable age. About aged three maybe, before it becomes intolerable.

"Not that Americans haven't got a lot to be angry about."

*

"OK, thanks for that," said The Stable. "I think it's your turn."

They weren't here to discuss politics. Or jazz. Or even Bob Dylan. Although it's not like they would ever meet up to do these things. Opportunity knocked! He knew that Monk was prone to rambling on incessantly. It had always been a habit, but since his accident in Spain a few years ago, it was much worse. The physical injuries were bad enough, but it seemed that his addled mind was now a permanent fixture. Monk was altered. Sometimes he just stared, vacantly. He reached to scratch his leg then pulled away spasmodically. It was difficult to watch.

Doberman didn't care for the impatience of The Stable; he liked Monk.

"I think you've got a point there. You should write it down."

"Oh definitely. If we chose all the highlights from our three decades of playing, we'd easily get a *Mr Men* book out of it. Mr Cards," Monk remarked with a degree of self-awareness.

"As if we're going to record all this shit," added Frazer.

Monk got bothered when people didn't engage. All he needed was a bit of recognition. His views weren't made up: they were arrived at.

*

8.00pm: rant continues...

"I heard a great quote the other day from another Nobel Prize winner, Harold Pinter, via the mighty John Pilger. You can look it up, it's worth it. During his acceptance speech, he summed up American foreign policy as: 'Kiss my arse or I'll kick your head in'. He elaborates somewhat, but that's the essence. More on it another day, I'm sure, but for now, hold your head and despair. It's hard to disagree when they're the only country who have murdered 200,000 civilians in a split-second revenge attack and would have carried on doing so until Japan fried like an egg. Easy over, yessir, goddam yellow-peril-motherfucker-war-ending US of A. Yeehaw! (Not sure how to spell that, but you get the drift. I've no time to check.) Look around and you'll see people painted in yellow and blue a lot, the same middle-class pricks who think that wearing a bobble hat changes the global mindset. There are people heaping plaudits on a comedian puppet who I can guarantee, didn't even know where Ukraine was on the map until last year. I reckon most wouldn't know where it is now! War is horror, all war; there is no glory, and it doesn't matter which bastard 'starts it' or 'finishes' it. War never starts and never finishes, we're all in it for ever thanks to the leaders we deserve. Propaganda and bullshit, for the most part: stop people thinking, by regurgitating Shithouse every pissing anniversary of every bloody battle in which some poor pawn got monstered by a monster. 'We'll fight them on the peaches [sic]' wasn't even recorded at the time of the parliament speech, or broadcast! The most fake collective memory of all was actually recorded after the horror in 1949, Churchill by then booted out of government in favour of policies beyond spouting jingoistic bullshit. On a greatest hits tour, his vast ego immune to pampering. Winston is the most overrated person in history as far as I can tell. English person, anyway. So sue me. Fuck Shithouse and his warmongering cadre. All I know is that if he, or Sputum, or pretty much any Potus you care to mention were on the frontline, there would be no war. I know nothing, but I know that veterans have no time for glorious victory. They were there. All wars are caused by the politics of greed. I've no issue with Sputum being on trial for war crimes. Provocation isn't an excuse, and all wars are a crime. He can get in line straight after Pubic and Hair. They had no provocation at all, ignored mass protests and, in their hubris, destroyed the United Nations. Goddam Ruskies aren't signed up to the ICC, though, chaps, nor are you in case you'd forgotten. In case 'Americans are disadvantaged'; in case justice is ever any more than an illusion. You couldn't make it up.

"I've gone off the American slant now, godammit! This was meant to be a piss take. So yeah, boy do I have some time for Americans, hell yeah! List your favourites now: King... Bradbury... er, Eastwood! I'm sure there are more. Carol Oates for starters, the Queen of the Night. I'll go back to that. But their gun laws are shit, their healthcare shitter and their foreign policy shittest. Shit, shitter, shittiest/never let it rest/til your shit is shitter and your shitter shittiest. If that hasn't been said before, I'll be surprised.

"So, we've got Bob (forgive me), Stephen, the gods of jazz, Ray, Joyce, Clint, and a few others. That's plenty for now. Maybe Yoda, although he doesn't strictly count. Is the Jedi part of the American Dream? No idea. The American Dream is literally bullshit. Propaganda again. And once more for luck. All countries do it, but we only hear about the American wet one because we're their jam boys in the East. Most great people are American, I'm pretty sure that's the case. Jeez, they would be, right? They speak the same language and there are lots more of them, so statistically it's inevitable. It's all about exposure, really. You can't expect me to know anything about great people who don't speak English. Are there any? Jesus Christ. He wasn't for starters. Although you wouldn't know it from most white boy, stained-glass windows. The church is good at propaganda too, got away with it for centuries. Now that it's died, I don't know that we're any better off. The sickle of secular sickness.

"We can go a bit longer, we're nearly there, but not quite yet. Oh yes! There was this chick, I nearly forgot. Of course there was. There's always time for a bit of sexism, right? Sure there is. Desire is sexist, by default. She had legs up to here; I never saw anything more serene and terrifying in my whole goddam life. Time stopped, time went backwards. I stopped breathing. I stopped existing. If things went on much longer, I'd be dead, or dying and puckering up for the kiss of life. It makes perfect sense. No one who hasn't died for love knows what it means to live for it. Sure, I could try some moves, I could move in for the kill, but I wasn't wired that way, I was too green, too redneck, too blue and too yellow. I was a pissing rainbow, dude. This chick (!) turned my way and she didn't want to know. Did I forget her? Of course not. You couldn't forget a thing like that. A thing like that used up more words. A thing like that you could hang your whole life on. Jesus Christ, if she'd only heard, if I'd only said something, then everything would have been different. That was the turning point, we'd shared a moment. On my side, eternity and the meaning of life. On her side, who is this prick staring at me? I'm, like, weak at the knees. I don't have any knees. I don't need them except for kneeling. To pray, or whatever."

*

The others were certainly praying – for this to stop. They had played a bit, but not enough.

"Are you feeling OK, Monk?" asked The Stable.

"What?"

"You seem even angrier than normal about American foreign policy tonight."

They were all used to his views on expansion and intervention.

"NATO is a good thing; it has secured peace in Europe for 80 years."

"Hell yes!" interrupted Dan. He couldn't sit by while his country was being maligned! He was ignored. Frazer glanced at him to make this clear. Monk might have been a tiresome tool, but he was their tiresome tool. They would rather listen to him, would rather listen to paint dry, than be introduced to a stranger.

"What are you on about? What is this cornflake packet crap! You can't prove a counter factual; you've no idea what would have happened without it. It's the American empire, nothing else."

"Infantile delusions about world peace are cornflake packet crap as well. Leaders on the front line? Yes, that would probably stop war, but the moon isn't made of cream cheese either."

"How do you know? Prove to me it isn't!" chirped Doberman.

"It could be stopped if people wanted to stop it! They're kept sedated and powerless by the endless propaganda and false promises."

Doberman laughed. "War is over! Imagine no possessions, says the man with three mansion houses and a private jet."

"People don't want to stop it; I think some people might actually like it. Keeps things simple," said Frazer.

"You can't be that cynical. If no one cares, there is no hope."

Frazer snorted. "There is hope, but no one cares about it."

The others left time for a short pause. Even his allies were getting impatient. They hoped that one day he would be saved.

Fat Henge was on his way. When he arrived, things would be OK.

*

8.15pm – rant continues, now internal.

I have to write in silence. Nothing else will do. The merest flicker of distraction sends me into spasms. Not, sadly, of the orgasmic kind. Damn dog barking again. If it does that one more time, I swear it's meat. Son of a whore postman won't put the letters through the door anymore because he thinks the dog is relevant. Bloody thing is more piss wind and no action than his owner, more likely to lick your balls than bite you. So, the letters get left stuck halfway into the bloody slot, like a diffident rapist and are rained all over by the time I get back from work. Nice. So, on the off chance that my identity hasn't been stolen during the day, I get to finger damp, wet bills. About as appetising as fingering damp, wet whatever. I'm thinking too many sexual references in that paragraph. Anyone would think I wasn't getting enough, which is self-evidently not the case. My wallet, if not my identity, was actually stolen in Germany last week. Now I have a real reason to hate the Krauts. But of course I hate them, I've been told to since I was in the womb! Since before then, actually. It's not like I can think for myself or anything.

Incidentally, if someone wants to steal my identity, then that is just fine. Like I give a shit. Want my identity? Have two. I've got several spare, if I can only remember where I left them.

Somewhere down the years, during the last period of my first marriage, I should think.

There was once a young man who believed in love. Now he believes in Miles Davis. Obviously, an exaggeration. He actually still believes in love but has no idea what that means now. Even if the people don't change, the love does. (A passing phase, see poets for details.) The simple purity of youth is clearly gone, as so many have realised before him, but that is not the point. The simple purity of youth is nothing but delusional bullshit anyway. Hormone-driven, primitive insouciance based on nothing more than having nothing to do and supported by the all-encompassing selfishness of the young. Why not be carefree when you have no cares? Try paying the mortgage when half your cash gets passed over with mutual loathing to your ex-wife, your unseen kids and her latest shag piece. Be carefree then and I'll buy you a bollock. Try being carefree when you've actually had something to fight against, when every waking hour hasn't been a cosseted exercise in class smugness, and I'll give you one of mine. That would solve a lot of problems.

Bollocks, by the way, is a mild English expletive. (Similar to 'Egad' -Ed) Heard my brother explain this to an American dude (huge, obviously) in Eastern Europe about 25 years ago. Amused me. Amused me a lot more than going to see Boris Godunov on the same trip. Jesus Christ, how dull! Fuck knows what the Yank was doing in Europe; the bastards are everywhere. North American Takeover Alliance, sign right here. Yes siren.

*

The problem was that Fat Henge hadn't arrived yet. Henge was a Fun Generator; without him there was no distraction except for Monk, and when he wasn't on form things sometimes got sour. If any of the others were in the least bit entertaining and didn't just sit around like moogs waiting for something to happen, it might have been easier. Still, it wasn't that hard.

Fat Henge would also form a natural barrier between them and the American noise machine. No one messed with Henge. One of his pet phrases was, 'You can go now, thanks.' His actual surname was Stone, naturally, which was already robust enough. He could probably have built the druid's temple on his own. It actually wasn't a druid's temple, of course, no matter how many Gandalf lookalikes waving golden sickles turned up to proclaim otherwise. Nor was it likely to be a clock, as far as The Stable was concerned. Who exactly would be able to navigate by it? And who needs a clock that large? Definitely a burial site. If Henge didn't arrive soon then they would have to take Monk there. Dig a hole.

*

Rant continues...

"Back to the steaming pile of irreverent corruption that we have become. Do what I say, or I'll hit you. Where is he? Shall I hit him for you? If that ball hits your car again, I'll come and tell you don't worry, then I'll hit you. Oh, grow up. I'm not going to grow up. I'm going to stand here and humiliate you in front of your son. You've done your best, now fuck off or I'll fuck you up. The language of the bully. The language of the thug. Bullies don't win? Of course they do! Crime doesn't pay? Of course it does, otherwise there wouldn't be any criminals. There are plenty in power, right? That's for sure. Don't believe them. They're liars.

"I used to be into politics after a fashion, but things have changed. The older I get the more I hate politicians. Or at least, the ones who lead them. Almost by definition you need to be a bastard to get on. It's not as if talent is a differentiator, any more than differentiator is a proper word. It's a real shame. Either they have become worse, thinner, even more self-serving veneers of human beings, or I've seen through them. Macaroon? He didn't even exist five years ago! Merkel seemed OK; I don't even know if I can remember the name of the new guy. Bidet – as bent as a nine bob note. Card-Shops? Get well soon. Jesus Christ, Crippen, I'll tell you what happened: Dump won because they could not stand the thought of you and your ilk again. Shove your tax dodging foundation up your twin arses, you odious pair of sanctimonious turds. The world would clearly be a better place with less American intervention! Or at least no worse and a lot less confusing. Global loan sharks. Stop leading the free world and let it make its own mind up. I, like, really believe that. So no, I don't mind Dump! He's obviously a crass, vulgar pig, but he's a pig who is happy in his own shit.

"And that will do for now. The American scream more like. Uh Huh."

8.30pm – rant over.

*

No one knew how many pauses there had been, they were innumerable. They were now, anyway, because no one had counted them.

"Will you just fucking play!" said Frazer. For a change.

"Oh sure, whose turn is it?" said Monk.

Doberman said nothing, just stared about him. The Stable sighed. It was a normal evening.

Even Dan seemed bored, but of course he could never stay bored for long. People like him never do. With all the sensibility of a cabbage, they assuage their own boredom by inflicting it on others. The endless repetition of a living vacuum:

"That's what I'm talking about."
"That's what I'm talking about."
"That's what I'm talking about."

The Crab

'Avoid loud and aggressive persons; they are vexatious to the spirit.'

Desiderata – Max Ehrmann, 1927

She had tried avoiding them, but after a time this became impossible. Increasingly irritated by the endless, loutish sound of others, she did indeed find her spirit vexed. People should just keep themselves to themselves. It didn't seem that much to ask.

Take this latest fat turd, who had rented a nearby holiday chalet. He did not need to leave his delightful, kind neighbour a threatening note stuffed through her letterbox because 'her dog kept barking and all he could hear was her radio'. Literally incorrect, since if the radio was all he could hear, he wouldn't have been able to hear the dog. And Radio 3 at that! Hardly strident; most of the time it was just tedious monks chanting. Or maybe they were thrilling monks, chanting tediously.

Arrogantly and deceitfully, he asserted that he'd come on holiday for some peace and quiet! Some peace and quiet with his own loud music pounding over a barbecue, while he bellowed jocular profanities towards his beer-swilling, bog-bowl buddies. He didn't even live here.

He had not needed to push in front of the line at the bakery, pugilistic and vulgar, while others waited their turn. And he certainly should not have abused the elderly gentleman who had objected.

"Piss off, pops, what are you going to do about it?"

She had been enjoying a cup of peppermint tea, for which she had queued. Sighing, she checked off her mental list, her imbalanced scorecard:

Oaf? Check
Loud? Check
Aggressive? Check
Appreciates classical music? No

This last one was optional, but she'd always thought that anyone who didn't appreciate classical music was subhuman. They didn't have to like it, of course, that was just down to taste, but they had to appreciate it had worth. They had to be aware of something beyond themselves.

It was really not looking very promising for Cabin Guy.

She could have issued a warning, of course, but that took time. People never learned and couldn't change. Better just to get rid of them.

*

The small boat purred, its electric Tornado motor all but silent in the black night air; the faintest ripple of a wake trailed behind. The moon was nothing more than a sliver, a celestial thumbnail pressed out of the darkness. Her night vision had always been exceptional.

At around 3am she gently nudged the riverbank. A sign threatened 'Private – No Mooring' but she didn't expect to be paying a fine. Disembarking, she secured her vessel with a highwayman's hitch, shouldered her bag of tools, and made her way to the cabin. One of so many similar buildings on the Broads, it was easily accessible by river and remarkably simple to get into, if you knew all the right buttons. She did. Quite often, a panel by the door could be eased open, if you pressed in the right place. If it couldn't, then plastic or wooden walls were not a major impediment. Just ask the three little pigs. Some of these cabins were little more than conservatories. It was also surprising how many people left their doors open – casual holidaymakers with no sense of ownership nor duty.

Once inside, she crept towards the main bedroom. She was very light on her feet, could have been a dancer. The man was breathing loudly, just short of snoring. He might have been showing early signs of sleep apnoea but hopefully wouldn't wake up. In any case, she was nothing if not quick. She had prepared 'the pincer' earlier, filling up the tiny tanks with this evening's heady brew. It was an ingenious design of her own making, a circular construction vaguely reminiscent of the device you use to cut foil from corked wine bottles. It clamped onto the victim's neck and delivered two simultaneous injections. Death was quick and painless, or at least it could be. Obviously, that wasn't always appropriate. Sometimes people needed to be admonished as well as despatched.

She reached towards the man and, as she did so, he moved. She froze, inhaling silently and holding her breath, which she could comfortably do for two minutes. His pudgy eyeballs moved slightly under the lids, as if slugs were trying to escape from inside his skull. In a trice, she attached her weapon of choice.

The man's eyes immediately popped open. He stared momentarily at his attacker, who was looking down at him disinterestedly. He instinctively tried to swipe at the pincer but managed nothing more than a spasm. He opened his mouth to scream, but noise was beyond him now. He died with a gurgle.

His body was found a couple of days later. On top of the bloating corpse was a pale purple calling card. It bore the silhouette of a crab in the top left-hand corner and a single word in the middle: *Vexatious*. In the bottom right-hand corner she had slashed a kiss.

*

The Crab acquired her name because of a slight limp that caused her to move sideways occasionally. Scuttling. This unusual gait had made her the object of bullying for a time at school. But then it stopped quite abruptly, and the bully was never heard from again. She was also a Cancer star sign and believed in the power of the heavens. They certainly had an influence over her. Whether being a water sign gave her a taste for the river, or whether she adapted herself to become more like her zodiac avatar, who knows. Like most things written in the stars, it could have been mere coincidence. But where was the fun in that.

The Crab worked in a lab, run by a Mr Zeus. He didn't blab. She sometimes got a cab; sometimes picked a scab if she'd inadvertently nicked herself during operations. He was an academic doctor but didn't like to brag or have to answer endless questions about piles. Having spent some time as a research scientist, he had eventually grown tired of the bureaucracy and retired to teaching, where he freely ignored it. He owned a small house near the beach and had no dependents.

Knowing that he could walk away at any moment made his second profession tolerable. Most of the fools didn't attend his classes anyway, and if those fools who did attend wanted to fill their pencil cases up with butane gas from time to time, what of it? That and dissolving things with acid were two of the greatest pleasures in chemistry. Titration looked interesting until the first time you did it. After that it was exceedingly dull. The liquid was pink, now it isn't. Great.

He had once been slippered at school for setting fire to an exercise book. It hadn't affected him that much, although he did wonder about a society that used violence as a means of correction. He wondered what it was saying to its young. All societies did at the time, so he was probably just wondering about human beings in general. All mammals did as well (probably), so he might have been wondering about them. He wondered what creatures who breastfed their babies and used violence as a means of correction were saying to their young. Not that all humans did breastfeed. After a while he stopped wondering – it was easier. Had he had children he could have run a controlled experiment. But never mind. These days, corporal punishment was outlawed, of course. 40 years ago, teachers could make hay while the sun shone. Most didn't, but there were always a few closet psychopaths around.

The Crab had first met Zeus on the beach, naturally enough, early one morning just as the sun was ambling its way into sight. He might have been posing as a statue; she might have been nibbling on mussels. Same process, different species. Let's avoid the snobbery. She was lithe and strong, maintaining this form largely through a regime of Krav Maga, extreme yoga and running. Not jogging, she hated that expression. When she ran, she ran. Extreme yoga was her own invention, which basically involved doing yoga with all your muscles clenched. Quite difficult.

Resting between sprinting bursts, she had fallen into conversation with this quiet, studious man and he had mentioned a job vacancy he had going as a lab technician. This presented various raw material opportunities, and she had duly applied. Zeus took great pleasure in giving it to her rather than the headteacher's nephew. She moved in and out of work like the tide, rarely settling in one role for too long.

She was the daughter of an engineer and good with her hands. She was particularly good at making instruments of death. She could have been an engineer herself but instead had chosen a different path, one that she was still on.

*

The thief had been lingering around the bike sheds for a while. Typically for an English winter it was dark, miserable and cold. But we all have to make sacrifices. He had his eye on a nice model, owned by another nice model who had recently started work at the hospital. Steal it, cycle home and then sell it to Calver. Easy money. Of course, if he'd only had a strong, positive male role model and a better upbringing he wouldn't have made the decision to steal. Apparently, only those brought up properly have freewill. The poor unfortunates who were not 'brought up properly' were just insensate drones, incapable of coherent thought. It was scarcely his fault at all. Devoid of his own volition, he literally had no other choice but to be an amoral, selfish prick and steal the bike.

Finger-snapping, knuckle-cracking and pop psychology aside, at that moment in time he had chosen to take something that was not his. It was entirely his choice, and others with precisely the same upbringing, improper or otherwise, might not have made it. The thief cut through the heavy-duty lock with some entirely unpremeditated, spur-of-the-moment, industrial-strength bolt cutters. If needs be, he would have returned the following night with an impromptu angle grinder and battery pack.

The owner was really chuffed with her new bike. It had been a graduation present from her ailing father, thrilled beyond words that he had lived long enough to witness his daughter's success. It was too bad that multicoloured governments had seen fit to charge her £40,000 in order to tend to the sick. It was too bad that the same governments didn't insist that developers put in enough car spaces for staff. It wasn't their fault either, they couldn't help it.

Two eyes had been following his progress into darkness. A figure stepped out.

"Is that your bike?"

"What?"

"Is that your bike?"

"Who the fuck are you?"

The figure remained silent. It shifted sideways slightly.

"Mind your fucking business, bitch. Of course it's my bike."

"I don't believe you. You're a liar."

"Fuck you!" The thief jumped on the bike and rode off. The figure followed. These new electric scooters were ideal for tracking, particularly once she had pimped them. She loved their silence.

*

The nurse finished her 12-hour shift, the third on the bounce. It had been tough: one death, one life, and dozens in between. It was amazing how quickly you got used to it. You had to, or you would go insane. You never became inured, though. If you did, then you would no longer be fit to care. The desire to alleviate suffering, to help, was a valuable and largely unrewarded thing.

She enjoyed cycling—it kept her fit—but it was a bit fresh in the winter. No choice though, the seven-year waiting list for a car space and non-existent night-time bus service saw to that. She'd be home soon and asleep.

She couldn't see her bike. She was sure she had left it there. Perhaps the next stall. Half asleep, her breath pluming in the iced air, she looked up and down the rows. She saw the severed cable and her heart sank. This was not what the doctor had ordered. *For God's sake.* She was tough but started to well up. Mercifully, it was time for an angel.

"Don't worry, I got it back for you! Some joker had a go at it. I persuaded him that was a terrible idea." The angel spoke softly, with the tiniest hint of some unknown accent. Perhaps Lisson Grove, or Prague.

The nurse smiled all over. In front of her was a slight, hench figure: pitch-black hair, somehow both tiny and tall. She was like a whip. The wrong person might have found her terrifying. The right person might have found her even more terrifying.

The figure adjusted its stance slightly, to change the weight from her damaged hip.

"Sorry about the lock, but you're welcome to this one. It's my own design."

"I, er... thanks! How did you...?" The nurse was too exhausted and overjoyed to speak properly.

"It's fine, don't worry. I was just leaving off."

"You work here?"

"No, not really. Sort of, from time to time. I'm mostly self-employed. I'll see you around."

"But... thank you so much. Lifesaver!"

The new lock had a small picture of a crab embossed on the front

The figure was already on her way. Normally secrecy was the thing, but sometimes it was nice to see happiness rather than horror in a stranger's face. She knew that the nurse wouldn't say a word.

*

The Crab made her way to the school lab. At the school gate was the usual crowd of uncouth youth. Their ringleader, Johnno, had been on her radar for a while. He had wilfully inflicted pain and suffering on others and would continue doing so. Highly vexatious. Johnno was an odious character who had spent his schooldays creating havoc, wanting to leave. The school had wanted him to leave as well but that process was virtually impossible to enact in the state sector. Inclusion was deemed the way forward, even if it meant diminishing the education of those who were not creating havoc.

Now that Johnno had finally left school, he hung around the entrance, grooming teenagers and threatening violence towards anyone who looked at him. He was clearly a sly, calculating predator, but that was difficult to prove. The interminably overstretched authorities took little interest. Occasionally the police perused and were reminded that it was a free country. Not free for people to enjoy untroubled lives, without fear of their children being lured away by delinquent vermin, but nonetheless free.

Johnno enjoyed impressing the young and impressionable; it gave him a feeling of power. He enjoyed scaring their necks with 'love bites'. He particularly enjoyed it when they were snooty, tall for their age types, like Charlotte. Her parents were desperate but could basically do nothing. Perhaps they were too liberal, and it was coming back to haunt them. They despaired of her suddenly hanging around with the 'wrong crowd'; they despaired of her looking like a woman when she was barely 15, but felt that trying to control her would be ineffectual and would drive her even further away. Perhaps they got it wrong. Perhaps they could not get it right.

The Crab looked at Johnno as she approached the gate. Malicious ignorance glared back.

"Yeah? What?"

She walked past him without flinching.

"I'm talking to you. Slant-eyed cunt."

They would be having words later. She would soon dissolve those layers of worthless aggression.

*

"How's it going, Doc?"

"Oh, mustn't grumble." Zeus rarely grumbled, there was little point. He didn't mind her calling him Doc.

"What can I get you today then, Vivian?"

"Just the usual, please. Nothing fancy."

He smiled. Her usual was fairly fancy. "Been busy?"

"Oh, you know, this and that. The rats are still a plague."

"Best I don't know, perhaps," he joked.

The lab work didn't take up that much time really. She had her own keys. Of course that was against the overweening bureaucracy, but Zeus wasn't one to worry about such petty foibles. Rules were indeed made to be broken.

The Crab was very much the exception which proved those rules.

The Theory of Fun

Abstract

Consider a social setting and an assortment of individuals therein. The aim of this paper is to allocate these individuals to buckets. We can do this literally, by carving them into chunks of perhaps offal, muscle, fat and bone, or figuratively, into mathematical buckets, also known as clusters, of similar groups. The literal approach is outside the scope of this document.

Discussion

This relates to the Special Theory of Fun as it pertains to small groups. Once social gatherings exceed a small number, say eight, then the General Theory of Fun for larger groups applies. Once social gatherings exceed a large number, say 50, then fun is impossible. At this point, total numbers must be stratified into smaller subgroups for analysis, which is likely to be made very difficult by cross subgroup contamination.

There are four basic kinds of people, four personality types, if you will. Obviously, there are shades of grey in there, but any social situation can be described in terms of these four types. Why people are the type they are is outside the scope of this document.

Clearly, there are more than four types of people. Categorise a second trait into four types and you'll immediately have 16 possible combinations. And so on. Depending on which way you want to slice the pie, you'll soon have more combinations than there have ever been human beings to fill them. Leave that to one side. When we talk of types, it goes without saying that we are talking about a particular context.

Fun Generators

The Fun Generator is the most well-known type. This type has three levels, from an entry Level One through to extreme Level Three. They are generally self-evident. These are the noisy ones at the centre of things. They are often the wilder ones; less concerned with acceptable behaviour, more concerned with having a good time. Having a good time is their *raison d'être*. These are the kinds of people who get things going, who are a laugh. Live wires. The kinds of people everyone likes, in small doses. Dickheads, in other words, but sometimes essential ones.

Fun Generators thrive on company; they have to be amongst people. A reaction is everything and they exist mainly to provide entertainment. They are the party-givers, the credit-takers, the people people, the clowns. Without, them life would be considerably simpler but considerably more drab. Usually, it is optimal to only have one Generator present, since they sometimes exhibit diminishing returns when in competition.

If a Fun Generator is not present, then others may be obliged to take up the role. This can be successful under clearly defined conditions, perhaps when people are gathered for a prearranged occasion or activity. In this case, the role of Fun Generator is to some extent already accounted for. However, it is commonly a disaster. There is nothing worse than enforced fun.

Since the finest fun is often spontaneous, Fun Generators are generally impulsive. Some have argued that they are best enjoyed sporadically. On occasion, it has been known for Level Three Generators to explode into a supernova of frivolity, covering everyone around them in the splattered gore of their outsized ego. Sometimes, keeping up with them is wearisome; sometimes, fun has the opposite effect. One woman's fun is another man's misery.

Fun Receivers

The second group to consider are Fun Receivers. These form the largest cluster. They are essentially foils for Fun Generators. There are two varieties of Fun Receiver: the Quiet and the Loud.

Loud Fun Receivers are characterised by belly laughing, rotundity, drinking and good-natured pomposity. Like the Fun Generators, they are usually sociable people; they enjoy being with groups. They like being in amongst it, whatever it is. They tend to have lots of friends because people find them genial, they are easy company. Who doesn't want to have their humour validated?

One occasionally finds pernicious Loud Fun Receivers in the wild. These are oleaginous sorts who bask in the glory of an odious Fun Generator and spread their poison vicariously.

Fun Receivers tend to need stimuli. If there are no people around, they will watch television, indulge in sporting activity or play with handheld devices. They need to be entertained and seek the company of Fun Generators for this purpose. They are loyal friends.

Quiet Fun Receivers are very different. They enjoy gatherings which are to their taste but they despise gatherings which are not. They are commonly extreme introverts and cannot abide large parties or noise. They are the supreme observers, missing nothing.

Fun Conductors

A more subtle group are the Fun Conductors. These are usually sarcastic individuals with a tendency to appear negative. They do not generate fun themselves, either because they are too shy or too distracted, but they embellish the fun generated. They amplify it, prolong it, and make it more amusing for the Fun Receivers. It is a covert role, not usually recognised. This requires a certain cynicism and a certain hatred of mankind. They tend to be lazy and wry.

Fun Conductors will often belittle other people, or events, or will mercilessly expose the ridiculous nature of things. They loathe pretension of any kind and will rage against it. They are connectors, but they tend to operate aside from things. They are not at the centre; they are the ones chipping in with bon mots. They are usually wittier than the Fun Generators upon whom they thrive, but lack the noisome, larger-than-life personality.

The role of the Fun Conductors is mixed, in so much as they also conduct mirth backwards and forwards between Generators and Receivers. Generally, they lean towards the Fun Generator, but they are equally popular with Fun Receivers. This is not just a hypothetical group of people who are too shamefaced or cowardly to be Fun Generators and too miserable to be

Receivers. The Fun Conductors are essential sidemen, operating in the margins of mirth.

Fun Destroyers

The last group are the Fun Destroyers. These people are quite rare. Most people can contribute something or are at least acolyte Fun Receivers who enjoy the good company of others. But Fun Destroyers contribute nothing. They devour fun. They suck the fun from a room, dragging it into a gaping black hole of boredom, thereby erasing all hope of happiness. A yawning morass of the mundane. They are immensely tedious, perniciously so. They attempt humour and fail, without recognising their lack of wit. The very worst of them criticise other people while adding nothing themselves, spreading a misery virus, infecting all who come near without any realisation. They do not take part. Such people are inarticulate, tedious, hostile and ill at ease. They are offensively unamusing, cataclysmically dull. They tell no tales.

But they cannot be ignored. If a Fun Destroyer is present, then the party is over.

General

The key thing is that for a great occasion, for a memorable event to take place, you require the first three types to be present. It is essential that fun is received and understood. Fun Generators on their own are merely vile hordes of loutish noise, desperately seeking an audience. Receivers on their own spend most of the time depressed, unless they are able to find endless new entertainments. Fun Generators and Receivers can operate in tandem for a while, but this puts a huge pressure on the Generators to be constantly creating new opportunities. They can burn out.

Fun Conductors are the most autonomous category and are contented enough on their own, up to a point. They can happily mock and sneer at the world around them; they don't particularly crave company. But without any society, without human contact, they eventually become embittered and lonely. A common combination is Conductor with Receiver. This almost works, but not quite. There is no spark. In a couple, one person may find the other hilarious, but hard work. The Conductor will become frustrated at the lack of raw material but lack the will to do anything about it. Unless the Conductor-Receiver couple find a Generator to spend time with, they risk a lifetime of frustration. Often the Receiver will run off with the Generator, leaving the Conductor feeling rather hard done by.

People don't generally realise this of course, but it is true.

Naturally, there are levels of expertise and levels of sensibility. As with all things, there is the issue of taste. Some Fun Generators will be nothing but a horror to some Receivers.

A Fun Generator might be a complete moron, in which case he should restrict himself to open mike nights in lager-only pubs. In some cases, he may have narcissistic tendencies or a very narrow field of influence. A Fun Receiver might be a genius, in which case she should seek Fun Generators of great style and substance. Nonetheless, at whatever level they are operating, the four basic types remain. There is a moderate bias towards male Fun Generators, particularly of the negative variety; there is a slight bias towards female Fun Conductors.

Another point worth raising is that people sometimes have a primary and a secondary type. For example, in certain situations, a particularly on form Conductor may find themselves a Generator, perhaps because they have stumbled on a rich seam of comedic material. Or a Generator may be unusually cowed, perhaps by family tragedy, and temporarily become a Receiver. More rarely a person might be adept at flitting between types, although such people are essentially modest Fun Generators. They are the consummate hostesses.

Everyone from time to time finds themselves being a Fun Destroyer, perhaps because they are in an unpardonably foul mood. Or perhaps because the company is either not at their level or is engaged in distasteful activity. In such circumstances the only sane option is to leave immediately.

Regardless of such transient departures from the norm, the primary type absolutely defines you and makes you the kind of person you are. In order to have any chance of happiness it is necessary to embrace this definition.

Conclusion

The Generator, Conductor, Receiver, Destroyer model as described by the Special Theory of Fun provides an excellent framework for the analysis of social groups.

Example

A group of friends have gathered for an evening of vague entertainment in the capital. In other words, an evening of sitting around complaining and failing to agree on a single political or religious point. They will at least agree that the price of a pint in increasingly outrageous.

Conductor 1: "Christ, beer is expensive now."

Conductor 2: "It's the tax. Bastards."

Receiver: "That's bollocks. Duty on beer is less than 40p and you can buy it wholesale for about £1.20 a pint. It's all mark up."

Conductor 2: "I read the other day landlords only make about 12p profit a pint."

Receiver: "Bullshit. Maybe after they've covered all their costs, bought a new car and paid themselves £100,000 a year. And they probably decimated their sales before declaring tax."

Conductor 2: "When you say decimate..."

Conductor 1: "If you're going to tell us yet again that decimate refers to Romans and killing every 10th mutinous soldier, I'm going to decimate you."

Receiver: "Profiteering, that's all I'll say. I'm not even opening it up for discussion!"

Conductor 2: "I'd like to see you get your fat arse out of bed and work for 12 hours a day."

Receiver: "Hardly my point. I'm sure they work hard, or at least their staff do, while they sit around scratching their balls."

Conductor 2: "I think he scratched his balls before pouring yours. Have a crisp."

Conductor 1: "In any case, £7 a pint is taking the piss."

Receiver: "Supermarkets are killing pubs, not the chancellor. And anyway, they're not dying. That's an urban myth."

Conductor 2: "They're all becoming shitty gastropubs, though. I'd rather smell smoke and armpits than chips and fucking gravy."

The Fun Generator arrives.

Generator: "Let's go to Cuba."

Conductor 1: "What, now?"

Receiver: "Great idea!"

Conductor 1: "Unfortunately, I've left my passport behind in Cornwall."

Generator: "We can pop and collect it on the way. It's only about a five-hour drive this time of night."

Conductor 1: "In what possible world is Cornwall on the way to London, from London?"

Generator: "God, whatever happened to spontaneity? Live a little! Fine, we'll go in April instead."

Conductor 2: "We'll need to be careful to avoid the Pope."

Conductor 1: "That should be easy enough in Cuba, I'd have thought. Thank heavens we're not planning to visit the Vatican."

Conductor 2: "There is a Papal visit to Cuba planned at some point this year. But I suppose we can always rearrange it."

Conductor 1: "Rearrange the Papal visit?"

Conductor 2: "I was more thinking our holiday, but whichever is easiest."

Generator: "Two weeks of sitting around smoking cigars and drinking mojitos sounds like our kind of thing."

Conductor 2: "Sounds appalling!"

Receiver: "Let's do it. What about the Destroyer?"

Conductor 1: "Oh, he can stay at home."

Further Examples

See elsewhere in the wider literature.

Fridya is a Level One Fun Generator. She tends towards the flippant. Joseph Storm is a Fun Conductor.

Doberman is another Conductor. The Stable is a borderline Destroyer. They await the arrival of Fat Henge, the Fun Generator, who will rescue them.

The Crab is a Quiet Fun Receiver. Although she is almost an exception to categorisation, she is certainly an observer. She is capable of slipping into Destroyer mode, but only when the fun being had is unacceptable – totally unacceptable.

Appendix

Optional formulation and gibberish (OFAG)

Special Theory of Fun (as applied to small groups)

Let Fun Evening (FE) = high, medium, low (categorical)

Where number of Fun Generators, Conductors, Receivers = FG, FC, FR respectively (integer)

Fun Destroyer (FD) = true or false (Boolean)

If FG >0 then if (FC and FR) >0 and FD=0 then FE = high

All three fun types present, no Destroyer. Optimal.

If FD = 0 and if FG=0 then FE = medium
No Destroyer present, but no Generator, so fun levels can only be medium.

If FD > 0 then FE = low (trending towards zero in the limit)
A Destroyer is present, so fun is not possible.

For high level Fun Evenings where FD=0, FG and FC and FR >=1 then

Fun Level (FL) = (2FC+FR) / FG (aka The Equation of Fun)

e.g.

One Fun Generator, two Conductors, two Receivers (and no Destroyers)

Fun Level = (2x2 + 2) / 1= 6

Two Fun Generators, one Conductor and three Receivers (no Destroyers)

FL = (2x1 + 3) / 2 = 2.5

If FG + FC + FR > 8 then apply the General Theory of Fun (large groups)

If FG + FC + FR > 50 then split into subgroups and consider infection rates

QED

Hard Pegging

1

The problem with this game is that it takes a long time to crush your opponent. He'd lost count of the faceless upstarts who thought it was just luck, who had fluked a few wins, won an irrelevant lower league and started mouthing off. The margins were fine and, of course, a top-flight player could be beaten by a clown. But not for long. In the end, the clowns stopped being funny. Besides, most of the real action happened outside the official auspices of Premier Peg.

Take this chump playing him now, whose quick decisions and cocksure, fluent manner belied a dearth of actual knowledge. Tiny decisions writ large. It was all about making those tiny decisions when your balls, sometimes literally, depended on it. If the cards were with you, fine. It was how you dealt with them hating you that mattered.

"You pegged loads," sneered his opponent. A sarcastic comment on poor scoring from the play phase, which was popularised by three gods of the game in the late 20th century.

Plunger smiled invisibly. This was a nothing game, of course, just a £1000 exhibition match alongside the main tournament. He tossed down his hand, a juicy combination of runs and 15s. "Sweet 16."

He marked the huge score on his favourite board. It had been fashioned from the thigh bone of a tiger and used sharks' teeth as pegs. Nice work. Drilling 121 holes into it had been difficult, but not as difficult as killing the cat with his bare hands then skinning it with his teeth. Obviously, that hadn't happened, but it might have. Having marked his initial 16, he flipped the box, which was also packed full of meat. It would be an easy win now. His opponent turned white.

"You might save the length."

The oldest English card game of cribbage has been around about 500 years. A lot longer than Americans, who of course, had tried to claim their own poker as the best card game in the world. Wrong! Sir John Suckling had allegedly invented it in bed, in Norwich. The best thing to do in Norwich is stay in bed, but then the same could be said of most places. Rather depends on whom you're with. Suckling was an inveterate gambler, rake, poet and idler. Hurrah! In his youth he had, allegedly, swindled the great and good out of millions, using marked cards. He would apparently send numerous decks off to various members of the aristocracy who were too gullible to realise something might be afoot. This eventually didn't go down well. Suckling died in penury, convicted of treason in absentia, after raising a fairly useless army of soldiers to support Charles I. Definitely backed the wrong horse, as things turned out.

Some of the proceeds, however, had been diverted and ended up accumulating into a large fortune, which had been used to bankroll the League of Peggers (LOP) in the mid-17th century. LOP was an appropriate acronym because anyone found cheating had a limb lopped off. This had almost certainly given rise to the cribbage term 'one for his nob.' Since then, the League had retained an elite, controlling presence. There was a pyramid structure, naturally enough, and the upper echelons formed the Premier Peg league of 52 players. They competed in matches to the death, from time to time, but there hadn't been one recently. The group generally flourished by rinsing newcomers, charging exorbitant fees, money laundering and running a black-market gambling syndicate. That saves a lot of explanation.

The rules of cribbage are well known and essentially involve scoring for different combinations of cards (including pairs, runs and totals of 15) as well as playing out the cards in a different phase of play. Some cards are discarded into a 'box' or 'crib' which counts for extra points. These various scores are 'pegged' by markers on a board with two lengths of 60 holes, the winner being the first to complete two laps. The board is pleasingly ergonomic and the method of scoring quite ingenious; each player has two pegs, and scores by jumping the back one ahead of the front one, thereby providing an easy check on the last score added.

In the unlikely event you're still awake, you'll be pleased to know that the dynamics of the game don't concern us too much more.

2

Plunger was also known as the King of Spades within LOP and a respected figure. Later that evening he found himself talking to Jake 'The Ram' Huggins about plans for the upcoming Crib Curdler. This was a massive event in the calendar, with one of the largest prize funds, and security was taken extremely seriously. Things usually ran smoothly but certain matters had to be addressed. Entry fees were significant; the exit fees could sometimes be even higher.

"How did it go?"

"Fine, no problems. He died in the hole."

Plunger had won a farm (no, really!) in a high stakes game some years ago. Among other features it had a well in the back garden. The previous owner had also been a Pegger (obviously, since otherwise he wouldn't have been betting the farm in a high stakes game.) Rumour, and indeed fact, had it that the well contained more than just water.

"Should have done what he was told."

"Never mind."

Plunger had quite enjoyed driving the brass peg into the man's right eye. So unnecessary. A simple branding would have been fine, but then things got out of hand. Best to take your lumps.

Davey 'Maximum' Sharp knew about taking lumps. He'd been branded as a young upstart, way back, following a disagreement about when to cut the pack. He'd been something of a hothead in his youth, but he'd learned how to behave and was now a loyal member of the security detail. Branding was a horrific punishment involving a red-hot iron shaped like a metal board. For artistic simplicity it only had five holes. It wasn't great having it pressed against your buttock of choice, but it was clearly way better than dying in the hole. People also had the option of having five cigars stubbed out on their skull. After sitting down and thinking for a while, Davey had gone for that option. Once his hair had grown back it wasn't that noticeable, but unfortunately, he had gone bald in his 30s and now wore a hat for special occasions. By and large, though, he wore his cribbage scars with pride.

As well as his head dimples, Davey sported various items of cribbage bling. He had a solid gold peg stuck through his right ear and his knuckles were tattooed with a Jack of spades and three fives. A fourth five (of spades) was inked onto his thumb. As everyone knows, five cards like that would score a maximum 29 in the game. Virtually unheard of, although Alice 'The Malice' Blackman claimed to have done it once, in her very first game. He joined Plunger and Jake at the table.

"Hey, Max, how's it going?" said Jake.

"Not bad, Ram, not bad."

They had known each other a long time. They'd first met in their 20s when playing in a Division Minus 50 pairs event. Division Minus 50 was the lowest entry-level tournament. Most players involved didn't know anything about the high octane, jet-setting world of cribbage beyond what they'd read in glossy magazines. They had been playing against a patronising old bastard and his wife, who had won by virtue of a ridiculous run of good cards. Their smug chuckling throughout was enough to piss off the Buddha. Afterwards, Mr Patronising Old Bastard had leaned over and offered some friendly condescension to the fresh-faced youths.

"'Don't worry, sonny, you'll learn."

Jake was relatively mild-mannered, most of the time. A collected individual, given to thinking. Davey not so much. He tended to favour the immediacy of outrage. Standing up, he had grabbed the back of the man's head and slammed it into the table.

"No, *you'll* learn!"

It had left a board-shaped indentation in his brow which would fade soon enough. Some diplomacy had been needed, but fortunately for them, the Patronising Old Bastard had been a long-term irritant to some of the elite players. No one minded a bit of frontier justice. The fracas had in fact drawn the attention and approval of the LOP cabal, which led to their long-lasting involvement. In the case of Jake 'The Ram' and Plunger, this was also a very lucrative relationship. Davey, lacking something of a brain, was more generally engaged on the enforcement side.

"So, I think we're all looking good for the Curdler,' opined Plunger.

The others agreed.

"Running like clockwork, boss," said Davey.

"Have most of the guests arrived?"

"Most. Alice hasn't shown up yet, but she will."

"She always did like to take her time arriving," said Jake.

Jake and Alice 'The Malice' went way back. Too far, probably.

"Heard anything from The Prick?"

"Not yet, but I expect we'll have to put up with him."

Peter Rickshaw, aka The Prick, was one of the most senior figures in LOP. He and Plunger had enjoyed various run-ins over the years. Fair to say they had different managerial styles. There was mutual tolerance because each knew how well-connected and influential the other was. But it fell some way short of respect. They were strong players and regularly traded blows in Premier Peg contests. Plunger had beaten him in the final of the Curdler event a few years ago, to his immense satisfaction.

They chewed the fat for a while longer, the kind of conversation that was both utterly pointless and utterly essential for certain groups of men.

"Better go and see to the draw, I suppose," said Davey. The draw was an elaborate affair and sometimes went on for hours.

"Catch you later, Maximum."

3

Alice was on her way. It took longer and longer now, but she was in less and less of a hurry. You couldn't always find the right partners. After tonight things would change. She'd been involved in the LOP scene forever, or at least as close to forever as made no difference. Having been willingly corrupted by Jake Huggins when they were both teenagers, she'd since led the classic cribbage rock and hole lifestyle: crippling stakes, cocaine-fuelled, all-night benders, the perpetual undercurrent of threat and extreme violence. It was a heady cocktail. Once you sampled its bittersweet taste there was no way back. Clearly there was, but it sounds more thrilling if there was *no way back*! She'd seen the future, and it was cribbage. She and Jake had parted company long ago but in many ways the passion remained, now morphed into a mutual lust for power.

For those who fell into the clutches of various sharks who loaned money to compete in the biggest events, there was certainly no return. Many fancied their chances and so were lured into the glamorous arena, but few succeeded. One of the biggest challenges had been the need to retain control of the empire and the rivers of gold that ran through it. The League of Peggers had created a monopoly, with a ruthless and often murderous dispatch of any group who tried to create a rival syndicate. To maintain this, you obviously had to make it pay, with regular backhanders to the people who mattered. Corruption worked. Locked away in the vaults were pictures containing all manner of debauchery, the great and the would-be-good lured into lewd propositions over an innocent-sounding hand or two. It was surprising what you could do with a crib board.

Broadcasting rights were tightly controlled. About 20 years ago, an odious antipodean had tried to muscle in. He'd gained the favour of various politicians and tried to buy up the rights to show every Premier Peg League game on a pay-per-view basis. The rewards offered were extreme for those who were tempted to sell out. But fortunately, wisdom had prevailed, and cribbage had remained a game of the people, for the people. It wasn't the national pastime for nothing. There was some suspicion that Peter 'The Prick' Rickshaw had been involved at the time, but fortunately for him nothing had been proved.

Recently, there had been murmurings about a new bid to franchise the League, which had led to those tensions which would hopefully be resolved later. Plunger had been clever; she'd give him that. But they'd given nothing away, no clue as to what might come to pass. They'd just have to see how it panned out.

4

The Curdler was in full flow. Davey 'Maximum' Sharp had crashed out but that was probably for the best since he was likely to be busy. Peter Rickshaw hadn't been seen since being dumped in the second round. Our other protagonists were still involved. The starting field of just over a 1000 had been whittled down to the quarter finals. Quartering finals more like. Of the eight, half were Premier Peg players. Plunger had drawn Jake 'The Ram' Muggins.

Alice 'The Malice' hung around like an upside-down bat, not used to playing the role of cribbage moll. She was a Pegger in her own right! She exchanged a glance with Maximum, who gazed back reluctantly. Jake surveyed the crowd, which had gathered round to watch this clash between two titans of the modern game.

"Before we start, I'd like to say a few words. Firstly, thanks to Plunger for helping to arrange this event which continues to be the most lucrative knockout event in the calendar. Secondly, he can suck my dick! He's a deck-dangling, bastard boy and his time has come."

"What the actual fuck?" spluttered Plunger. This was indeed unexpected.

Deck dangling meant tampering with the cards in some way, to gain an edge. Cheating. It was unthinkable that someone in the upper echelons of the game would resort to it. Plunger started to stand up but felt an unyielding hand clamp down on his shoulder. The hand was adorned with jacks and fives.

"Max, what the hell?" There was no point trying to shrug him off.

"I didn't have any choice, boss," said Davey Sharp.

It was basically true. Once he'd been told what was going to happen, there was nothing much else that needed hearing. At that point he was loyal to both parties, but that was no longer going to be possible. Neutrality wasn't really part of his make-up. Besides, it would have meant exile. He could have sided with A or B, but there was no way to side with both. There was also no way to side with neither, because he needed to stay on the inside. In Davey's straightforward mind, it was as simple as that. It had been a tough call, really. He had nothing personal against the King of Spades, but Alice and Jake went way back.

"The thing is, Plunger, we know what you've been up to. The Prick told us. Not that I'd trust him to look after my toenails. I didn't trust him 20 years ago either. But he was helpful – he got us access to your well-kept records. We know that you've been planning another sell-off. It wouldn't have succeeded, they never do, but we've had enough of you squatting up in the farm like a scheming fat turd. It's time for some fresh blood."

"Fresh?" cried Plunger. "You're about as fresh as an unwashed fanny! I'm not listening to this. Get on with the game or piss off."

It wasn't going to work. The Malice had spent weeks doing her thing, whispering and screaming as required. The game was up. He had been respected but never liked. Both were necessary. There was only the last option available to Premier Peg players.

"I demand the Final Cut."

5

The Final Cut was a ritualistic execution, available to certain members of the Pegging elite who were found guilty of crimes against cribbage. As well as choosing the means of one's demise, albeit randomly, it leant a certain pomp. It also gave the condemned a limited chance of reprieve. The condemned had to cut a card from 'The Deck' which was an ancient pack fashioned from dragon leather and passed down through centuries of exaggerated myth.

All the black cards meant death. Clubs represented suicide in increasingly dramatic fashion: head on a train line, glass of hemlock, and so forth. Spades meant being executed in one grotesque form or another. The full details need not concern us but included relatively benign examples such as being buried alive or guillotined, alongside more imaginative swansongs like live pickling. Being lowered feet first into a meat grinder was a particular favourite of Davey, who tended to pick up the execution detail. Red cards were somewhat less fatal. Diamonds meant incarcerated servitude without honour, which was probably not preferable to death. For instance, having to lick clean prison toilets before breakfast. Hearts offered various forms of penance, before exile to insalubrious domains.

The League of Peggers didn't concern itself too much with appeals. Due process was served by the horrendous fate that awaited anyone found guilty of a false accusation. Without too much ado, the dark army of Curdler players gathered in the circular theatre that was also the setting for the final match. That would still be concluded, later in the evening, once this tiresome distraction had been dealt with. It was a perfect viewing arena, everyone close to the action.

Plunger sat strapped into an oaken chair, hewn from a gigantic, clifftop tree which had been vandalised long ago. Members of the Premier Peg elite sat around a long, gnarled table. Alice unwrapped 'The Deck' which had been brought down from its museum plinth, where it usually sat alongside various pickle jars and other cribbage memorabilia. The audience members were rapt. For some, this was their first experience of the Final Cut. A susurration of voices began, gradually building in frenzied anticipation.

"The deck," started the chanting. "The deck! The deck!" they roared. Hands slapped thighs, a dull, pounding accompaniment. A drum roll of doom.

The pack was passed around the elite members who each gave it a prestidigitator flourish. It was then shuffled in the flipper, an old mechanical device. The Malice, as chief prosecutor, cut the deck and placed the top remnant face down. She picked up the next card and held it aloft. There were gasps among the assembled throng as she revealed it to the room.

Fenris

At the end of all days, he will be released from his chains and burst forth to wreak savage revenge on those who dared to bind him. This monstrous spawn of Loki, lashed to a rock with the iron rope Gleipnir, fashioned by dwarves from obscure ingredients such as the footfall of a cat and the breath of a fish, will at last be free. Another ingredient was the beard of a woman, which is perhaps not as obscure as the ancient Viking bards thought.

Vast jaws, which stretch from Heaven to Hell and can swallow moons, will devour Odin the Allfather of the Gods. Odin will be avenged by his very long-armed son, who will rip the jaws apart and plunge a spear deep into the wolf's evil heart. A brief reprieve before the earth is engulfed with lava and the whole world burns.

Good times!

Fenris Wolf was one of three children, born of Loki and a giantess called Angurboda. The other two were the fun-loving Midgard serpent and a fiend called Hel who is forced to preside over the underworld. One half of her body is described as rotting, the other half alive. Unsurprisingly, the alive half has a downcast expression. There is only so much making your house a home you can do in the underworld.

The Norse gods didn't like Loki's dalliance with a giantess, despite the fact that Odin himself had a giantess first wife called

Jord, with whom he had fathered Thor. Sauce for the goose was not sauce for the gander in Asgard. Without these dubious double standards they might have avoided a lot of bloodshed and been much duller. Separating destiny from luck is notoriously tricky, but Odin had to marry Jord because the talking head, Mimir, told him to. If you carried around a talking head in a bag, then you'd listen to it as well.

Legends are not there to be taken literally. That is not the point. They are there to carry eternal force, carved out of history.

Fenris is obviously the most agreeable of the three children, who were uncharitably described by the other gods as monsters. He is also the one who looks most like a dog. Hence an inevitable name for the family pet. Their own Fenris was much smaller.

Father and son picked him out of a pile of puppies presided over by Jack of Cost, the breeder of hell-hounds from a town in the East. Cowering behind a flowering sofa, steeped in the odour of a million curs, he peeped out. His siblings were unkind to this runt of the litter; they excluded him, bit at him, pushed themselves forward for selection. The young boy thought for a moment and then selected Fenris, a natural bias towards the underdog showing, even at this early stage. They had named him in advance. It was foretold.

*

Many tales have been told about Fenris; all are at least partly true. His escapades included plunging into a burning bush to savage a chicken, returning with feathered lips and wild eyes. His bark was loud enough to bring down walls, though it was not loud enough to scare Guinness, a cat from another world, who strolled past him one day into the kitchen. Glancing dismissively before sniffing the evening feast, deciding against eating such filth, and strolling back out. All bark and no trousers.

Fenris liked to torment socks, ripping them from the feet of passers-by, growling and slavering. Only the young girl was able to persuade him otherwise, with a roundhouse move learned from the retired podiatrist Bunions, corn shaver of the gods. He once roared under the forbidden gateway of Gunger-Gash in order to attack a violent Alsatian, before roaring back with a different view of his own mortality, punctured in both ego and backside.

He ran 1000 miles to keep up with a singer; was wrongfully released from a furnace by a forest witch in Norfolk; licked mountains of salty hands into the shapes of leaders. He was terrified into silence by the giant caterpillar, Dachs. No creature could behold Dachs without being horrified by its slow, revolting and all-consuming movement. It might crawl over you, or through you, brushing its dead hair against your own stale flesh.

There were many tales of the wolf but only one on which to linger here.

*

The dog had always hated the sound of hooves. No one knew why. Perhaps it had faint memories of Sleipnir, Odin's eight-legged flying horse. Another theory is that it was a throwback to less ancient cattle-rounding behaviour, passed down and still buried in its genes. The man had seen one of the same breed doing this once in Romania. Real life folklore. Whatever the reason, Fenris became a fury whenever horses were near, flattening himself against windows and scattering the gathered ornaments of decades.

On that day many things happened together to create the catastrophe: the killing of Fenris. He was lost to them in the blink of an eye.

They lived on a hill of sorts. (More of a slope.) On the other side of the road was a graveyard. It was a common rat-run, riddled with cars and other vehicles. This was particularly true at school times because of those too idle to walk their children, or for trespassers who lived too far away to do so.

It was the hill down which the girl first walked out of sight, one year ago. He could remember it distinctly. Not gone long, but still, the first rending of parental jurisdiction. On this day, all were at home except the mother. She was at her studio, fashioning a wedding dress from unicorn fur.

The man opened the front door to the sound of hate. Horses rarely used the road, and it would have been inane to do so at this time of day, given the multitude of cars and lack of any nearby pasture. Nonetheless, there were horned feet around. *Clippity-clop, clippity-clop.* Like coconuts at a nativity. Before the man could slam the door shut, there was a blur of fur. A black, raging streak hurtled out of the doorway. A cannonball of piratical intent.

Miraculously, his son was in the driveway. The boy was tall and had a long way to reach down. He grasped vainly at the collar and managed to hook one finger over it. Not enough. The dog bolted away into the road, towards its doom.

There were two screams. One from the horse as it reared away, and one from his daughter, who knew what must happen next. A desperate screeching of tyres and a sickening thud; a wet crunch. Far too loud to survive. The girl looked at the man in frozen horror, her face stricken. Time ceased, everything turned into slow motion, a crippling gravity of inertia. Their senses seemed to shut down as that small part of the world ended. They were drenched in a cacophony of silence.

The boy lay on the ground after his final, desperate lunge. His clenched fist clasped a clump of black hair. The girl held her hands to her face.

*

Pain.
Blackness.
Falling. No bright lights here.

Geat, zleep, rhag.
Smelling, fouling, eating, growling!
Fear. He didn't like it here. Half formed mistress. Now, now where was Master?
Panic, bark, terror, spark.
A roar of fire, burning.
Now, now, everything was present. Everything is present.
It could hear the screams. Felt numb.

The dog could articulate nothing. It had only senses to feel with, communicating with scent, touch, taste. No communication here, only fear.
Emotional intelligence, genius level.
Lost somewhere else. Never to be found.

Something shambling towards it. Something that contained only emptiness.

Smelling, fouling, eating, growling!
Geat, zleep, rhag.
The dog could articulate nothing, but it knew.
Darkness. Whimper. It needed comfort.
It turned to face down the horror.

*

As despair struck them down, there was a new sound: a rippling of the air as fate itself was twisted into a new shape. History would fall one way or another according to that moment of immortal rupture. The rock of ages had been hewn. Somehow, from somewhere, Fenris was coming back. His tongue lolled, crazed and foaming. There was a deep gash in the side of his head. Madness danced in his eyes, for he had seen things no creature should see. With one leg dangling behind, he forged his way to salvation.

Mercifully, the car had slowed down to go past the horse and so had crushed the dog less effectively than it might have done. The skilful rider got their horse under control. No harm done. Not to the horse, anyway. The driver got out. He was frantic.

"Oh, God, is… is he OK? I'm so sorry, he came out of nowhere. I've got a little one myself."

The man gathered up the dog; the girl rushed to comfort him.

"Fenny Boy!"

"Jesus, that was close," said her brother.

"He seems all right, not wincing much. Hopefully no internal bleeding. Let's get him to the vet."

So Fenris lived to fight another day. In fact, many more. He was a mighty 17 before he finally went to join his kin in Valhalla.

*

He was just a dog. Not worth a single hair on the worst human head. That's that we are told. That's what we know, objectively. 'Anthropomorphism is bad', bellows the atheist preacher, missing the point entirely. I know that rabbits can't talk. And yet, I'd rather believe in them than believe in you. At least some of the time. We're not all made of chalk.

Projecting our emotional needs, perhaps even the best of ourselves, onto another entity is not the act of a simpleton, it is an act of love. Foolishly, we see ourselves mirrored in adoration. Foolishly, we believe.

At the end, we let them go out of love, not because we want their basket. Perhaps one day we will be allowed to make the same decision for human loved ones. A few unscrupulous, criminal minds will take it as an opportunity to gnaw on a new bone. They would, anyway. Most will just want to preserve the best of what remains, at the end of all days.

Of course, he was just a dog. But he was also a legend.

Bingo

1 (On Its Own)

It is never very clear when it gains form and stops being alone. Or at least beyond the intimate company of one. Certainly, at some point there is volition, before that there is nothing. Not even yet the will to live. For me, one choice trumps another whichever way you look at it.

Bingo halls were never her Mecca. But once or twice on a wet afternoon it had been known. The fug of smoke, the tutting fury of old women when you dabbed too loudly, the dreadful odds against winning. Better off doing the pools. Worst still the fake call! A forced shriek of pleasure, the public humiliation. She (the grandmother) had stopped going at all when expecting him. Smoking was part of the fun, part of the ritual. It gained you membership of a tribe. Native smokers. She also stopped drinking except for a single bottle of stout on a Friday night. For iron.

The smoke had gone now, of course, and with it the rest of the atmosphere. Hygiene had replaced the lure of seediness. But the randomness still appealed, the endless search for meaning. Generations of time tripped up in stages, overlapping.

11 (Legs Eleven)

The boy had always enjoyed playing games. Board games, after a fashion. Classics like Risk and Monopoly were the best because everyone knew the rules. He didn't like rules much, they were the worst part of any game. Even from an early age he was resistant to new rules, or rather any authority that imposed them. Cards and dice were much better than boardgames. They were serious, grown-up things. He liked that people couldn't understand randomness and seemed to blame everyone except themselves for their own bad luck. There is no such thing as luck, in the end.

Of course, there was a great deal of luck in individual moments, but it tended to even out. And if it didn't that just wasn't fair. No one ever said it was going to be fair. Indeed, fairness is the greatest lie, the grandest myth of all.

22 (Two Little Ducks)

He (the son) woke up badly that day, to the inane twittering of birds in the tree outside his window. Sleep had been departing early for some time now, although perhaps he still spent as much time in slumber without the limb-twisting preamble he had abstained from, monk-like, for the last six months. Since she'd moved out of his life there had been nothing between the sheets, nothing between the lines. He had tried, too hard a couple of times, but found himself avoided fairly quickly, regretting his own weakness.

It was a full life, no doubt of that. He had limited excuses for self-pity and no reason to doubt himself. Everything that had happened, which had been so monumental and yet so ultimately irrelevant, had happened with his approval. Some things are approved in too much haste, that is all. But he had never once acted without feeling that he was doing the right thing. Even when saturated with guilt and anger, raging against the injustice of fate, he had felt that he was right; that it was the world, not he, at fault. It wasn't so much arrogance as contempt, that finest of lines. He did not feel better than others, just more able to see them for the shit they were. He held himself in similar high regard.

He was not a people person. He was dismissive of his fellow man but could not understand why everyone else did not feel the same revulsion at this rank stench of existence. The sheer endless, mindless, noisy intrusion of other people into his own space, his own time, was on occasion too much to bear. With a clattering of bricks and an artificial scream of horns, braying a cretinous welcome to other dumb fools too ignorant to care, they thrust their brainless forms into his world. Oh yes, it was easy to hate. It is surely impossible for the intolerant not to hate.

He had tried to tolerate other people, of course. Sometimes he even grimaced at them. It wasn't that he was unsociable—on the contrary—merely that he did not seek company. He enjoyed comfort and a lack of change. Old friends, hidden smiles, secrets and shared histories were fine. But not small talk, not idle chitchat. That was for the birds outside his window. He needed other people, though, he did get lonely. He liked to rail against the prevailing view, liked to argue, to answer with barbed sarcasm, to joust and spar and belittle. Not spitefully, but in a mocking tone.

Only sometimes did his tone become savage, for he had a temper behind his eyes. There was a thunder about him. Not a threat of physical confrontation, never that, but a dark cloud of hostility, the hint of a livid storm only just held at bay. A murderous quality. In the minute intake of breath, an imperceptible setting of teeth you could see, if you knew too well for your own good, the war going on beneath the surface. This battle could be lost at any moment and erupt into a destructive, slavering rant, words more violent and more crushing than any fist.

Many hours had been spent trying to understand why he had this superficial loathing of everyone and this genuine loathing of most. These were hours spent alone, of course, since to seek professional help on the subject would have been akin to sprouting wings. Some things are not in our nature. Despite much thought, he had failed to come up with anything other than the most fatuous generalisations, none of which shed any light on his manner. Since interpersonal hostility is unlikely to be a desirable hereditary trait, it seemed implausible that it had been acquired naturally.

*

His childhood had been more or less idyllic, with the usual veneer of strife. Nobody likes to admit they have an easy life. Admittedly a generation back his family had been solid working-class stock. His grandfather (the great-grandfather) had been a labourer in the vaguest sense, and perhaps his good-humoured idleness had been the unconscious catalyst into the relative middle-class decadence that, as a child, he had enjoyed. His parents had aspired to 'more' and shared a work ethic which appeared to have skipped a generation. He had been brought up to know the value of money, by God. Whilst they had certainly not been poor, there had been a constant awareness of the value of money.

This was one source of parental friction and there had been others, which led to the mild undercurrent of conflict that had abounded. Mainly verbal, with occasional hurling of blunt objects. A lot of argument, sometimes good-natured but often not. Some exposure to emotional viciousness and a vague whiff of vengeance in the air. Excessive discipline laced with none whatsoever. But these things were of no import. His family had been an enormous support and a bedrock over the years.

Siblings had been enjoyed with a fairly standard combination of competition, hatred and love. There was no ongoing rivalry or unhealthy residue. Each had grown and lived and been apart while still together. One day this would change, but for now there was nothing in that.

Later childhood, at school, had largely been splendid. Throughout primary and middle schools, he had been almost a prodigy – hugely bright and ahead of his peers. Perhaps that explained a certain distancing and aloofness of nature, but he had since rationalised this and did not see his intelligence as a sign of superiority. It was just a fact in itself that made him more capable and more complete than others in some areas. He was remarkably incomplete in others. High school at 13 began with some mild, good-humoured bullying but this had been dealt with in customary head-on fashion. An element of spite was only to be expected at a high school and had not moved much beyond day-to-day bawdiness. Whether it was inspired by envy or self-adulation, he did not know.

He was an odd combination of sublimely confident and very awkward, depending on the situation. This variation of manner seemed imponderable. There were no common themes which determined whether a situation would be comfortable or not. Perhaps he was mildly depressive and was best left alone at such times. Certainly, there were times when people were superfluous. He only had so much joy to give.

But he was a good man; a misunderstood man. A man whom people loved but could not love. A man who felt no jealousy but inspired it without ever knowing why.

33 (Dirty Knees)

I (the friend) didn't know much of this until later, when I had pieced together the various facets of his character and heard much about his mind. He became, eventually, a very great companion and yet I could never quite understand his pain. I think there was something lost, something very far beneath that he had all but forgotten himself. Or at least had buried way, way down. We had good reason to be close, for we loved the same person. In those situations, you either become close, you win or you die.

44 (Droopy Drawers)

Eventually, he (the son, now also a father) concluded that he was a fantasist; that his epic thoughts and epic feelings would not translate eventually into some noble cause. In fact, these epic feelings amounted to nothing that anyone else was much interested in and, moreover, did not even touch the object of their affectation. That is not quite true. They touched her beyond words. They had known love, and they knew it still. But she (the muse) had made her choice, and she remained steadfast in it. His words had failed him, had in the end changed nothing.

Did words ever change anything? He had thrown everything he had at her. Portentous his words may have sounded but portend they did not. Not in this age, anyway. He was ahead of his time.

Everyone is hiding from life, of course they are! To stare it in the face would be unbearable; to embrace this awful reality would be too much. Its pettiness, its squalor, its grandeur are all but stages. The only way to bear it was to find some secret corner, some sanctuary. God help him who tries to take on the world at its own game. The best you can hope for is greed; the worst is damnation. The lush in her corner is no different really to the addict lying in his gutter. Both are trying to escape reality, to escape the mundane. One is more acceptable than the other and better funded, that is all.

*

Once upon a time he had found 'perfect love'; he had been completely revealed to this woman who even now, some 20 years on, remained his muse. Did such a 'perfect love' need to last for ever? Probably not. But this was as near as it got. When does an infatuation become worthy? When it is reciprocated, presumably. When it is requited. When all that stands between yourself and eternity is the present, even if it cannot be overcome. When does a sick obsession become wonderful? When it is both cured and proved, of course! Could it be any more obvious than that?

Anyone can admire from afar. Anyone can do anything to anyone from afar. But what they had was real, there was no doubt of that. His fantasy was only in the endurance of his affection. There was no possessiveness about their relationship at all. He had become 'involved' with her when she was seeing someone else. He accepted that and did not care. His attitude towards her incumbent had been, bizarrely, one of complete disinterest. There was no family involved – that would have been different. There was not even a marriage involved. That also would have been different.

Her incumbent didn't protect what he had. He could so easily have done. She was lonely and yet to embark on the rest of her life, so in this hiatus of indecision they had weaved their unique relationship. It was to remain frozen in time; it was to remain 'perfect'. They had fallen in love, it was as simple and as awful as that. He had lured, but never threatened and, in the end, he had been beaten.

Nothing had happened.

In the end she had been unable to tear herself away from expectation and upheaval and doubt and yes, love for another. Whoever thinks that it is only possible to love one person at one time is a fool. To take Anna Karenina's remark a step further, there are even more ways to love than there are hearts. She (the muse) was an immensely kind person who had found herself in an impossible situation. It must have been dreadful for her. When forced to decide, she had chosen the easy path. Perhaps she had been forced down the easy path.

That was half his life ago. Now, there was not a single day that passed when he did not wish he had announced himself. He could have shattered the illusion. But to do so would have meant that he became less. In attaining happiness, he would have brought sorrow. It was partly the dignity of his acceptance that made her realise she had made the wrong choice. Sadly, she did not realise this until too late.

She thought of others more than she thought about herself. She did not live through her children, but she lived for them. She never bragged vicariously, but she breathed their welfare. She was the 'perfect mother': underrated, selfless, and totally, unrelentingly a fury for her young.

This trait, of always placing the concerns of others before her own, had led them to this position. He was the interloper, the madness. His needs had to be less than the needs of the person she was with, it was as simple as time. He had done all that he could, and it had almost, almost, been enough. Did he have the strength to take on that burden of lost hope again? Or was she right, that the past should stay in the past?

But to look into her eyes still, on rare occasions, and see the collapse of boundaries, the immolation of self and the infinite sadness of hope – that was enough to sustain him. Her eyes were the only journey he had ever needed to take. He had drowned in them many times and would do so again without a moment's thought.

She had a particular way of regarding him when he needed help, a look of total understanding and empathy. She would smile, slightly, as if she was a child, the innocent and pure reflection of complete, unquestioning knowledge. A gaze, saturated with kindness, would fix him and hold him there. She would protect him until the next time he needed a friend. She was his idol, she was his every day, she was his casual glance. She was his truth.

*

This is more or less what he thought. On a good day. On a day when fantasy ruled. On a bad day he wondered why he had been so dignified, so noble. Why not destroy and maim? Why not ruin everything for her, since her own inertia had ruined everything for him! But these were absurd specimens of bitterness, not worthy of him. Had he talked then, the pain he inflicted on her would never have been soothed. Better that there is only one person in pain than two, surely? Of course it wasn't fair, but what of that? No one ever said it was going to be fair.

On a good day, he was glad that they had stayed close, that they had an understanding. Sometimes she even came close to admitting that she'd made the wrong decision, all that time and life ago. But that wasn't accurate. It is all too easy to decide things after the event. His own life had continued and had once been full. It was empty now, if emptiness is measured by attachment. But he had loved again, he had watched children born and attempted to build a home. He had remained on good terms with the mother of his children and would continue that friendship. It was still a good marriage, despite being over.

Indeed, if current events were anything to go by, it was clear that there was really nothing his ex-wife could do that would ruin that friendship. Friendship is, after all, fairly straightforward. There are rules that anyone can follow. You don't lie; you don't cheat. You share everything that you want to share and ask about nothing else. You're there, you're not there. You can always be relied upon when the shit hits the fan, but you don't need to go looking for it. Most shit you can just ignore. Friendship is easy, there are no expectations and, when a friendship ends, it doesn't undermine everything you thought you stood for. It's just a misunderstanding that gets forgotten when people regain their perspective. Not like a marriage. A failed marriage is a failure of fantasy, of dreams. Probably not before time, in his case, but nonetheless it represents a partial unravelling of childhood.

The demise of his marriage, and his part in it, had confirmed to him something that he had always known in his heart: the grass is not greener on the other side of the fence, the grass is never greener. Whether dying or covered in dung, the grass is brown everywhere.

This was essentially the position she (the muse) found herself in now. After she had made her decision, or at least not altered the decision made for her, she had enjoyed all the trappings of a successful life and continued to do so. She was, if she didn't think about it too much, entirely fine. But she was caged by the freedom of others. Organising everyone else's complacent happiness left little time for her to organise her own.

It did not occur to her that her children would one day vanish. That was unconscionable. Why would you need to move away from the foundation of all in/security? (Delete as appropriate!) What greater blessing/curse could there be than the balm of un/conditional love? She was not necessarily naive in this view. Many families stayed close, physically as well as emotionally, and supported each other, to some degree, throughout generations. But it is not the modern way. These times in which we're obliged to live demand more space. Even the most devoted spawn can find itself on the other side of the world.

She loved him still and the fantasist was sure of that. But she placed her family first and her only fear was that something might threaten this. So, to a large extent, she avoided the risk. She felt that at any moment her feelings might spill over, that some great chaos could descend and ruin what she had built. She feared that the ice that separated them from their past might break, that they would plunge, floundering into the black waters of imbroglio, leaving the lazy comfort of their lives behind. It was a reasonable concern. There is nothing more selfish than love, after all.

*

For 22 (*quack-quack*) years now he had continued his life, she hers. Always he had been available to her, always she had resisted. He was ordinarily a person who felt guilty. His vague and disorganised religious notions had imbued a certain morality whilst at the same time allowing a wide latitude for interpretation. Infuriatingly, he was moral enough to have a shit time on Earth but not moral enough to get into Heaven. He felt somebody was to blame for that, somewhere along the line. In a cage, you either learned to love the bars or tried to escape. The situation was at least clear. A moral cage with an open door and a comfortable sofa was confusing.

Strangely, he had never felt guilt about his dealings with her. None at all. They had their own rules. On the few occasions they had talked alone, he had tried to make this point. She more or less agreed, but never entirely. They never had enough time to dwell on the subject, nor quite enough moments gazing into each other. Not quite. He felt to the core of his being that she yearned (or at least yawned) for him while holding herself back. Her self-restraint was cursedly admirable.

He respected her stance and accepted it. Always a good position to adopt when you have no choice. He longed for her to one day return to the person he believed in, but did not think this would happen. At least not until they were both too old to care or act. From time to time, he wondered why they bothered to maintain any special closeness but quickly realised that they had no other option. Any frustration was soon enveloped in friendship.

Was it healthy, this continued reference to their past? These emotional monuments to years for ever gone risked becoming an empty cause. To what extent had they not 'moved on', to employ that vulgar phrase? What, exactly, was so great about moving on when it left behind such savage regret? Injustice has long arms. Injustice can suffocate. It can also drive you mad.

In the end, indecision was snatched away. Her husband ran off, literally, with an Egyptian belly dancer called Fatima. We plan; God laughs.

55 (Snakes Alive)

They never died. He (the son) reunited with she (the muse). Charming pipes, weird baskets and a recalcitrant reptile.

It had taken most of a lifetime, but they did eventually find their way back to each other. A triumph of time. Nothing was the same, nothing ever could be. Patience, that virtue so overrated that it turns into a sin if you wait long enough. There was joy, companionship and comparison. He didn't like being compared to other people, unless it was favourably. But he supposed that occasionally it was inevitable. She didn't do it very often. There was disappointment at the wasted years but, of course, that was an idiotic, vainglorious simplification. Children cannot ever be a waste, unless they grow up to kill you with an axe. Nor can fond memories.

They had reunited late, almost too late. But for once, love won. It was a tired and aching love, one which had perhaps left its finest days behind. There was plenty more to come, though; this bold passion, this lifesaving grace.

66 (Clickety Click)

Creaking limbs and leaking fatigue.

Late divorce (the grandfather). Worse than early. There is no time limit on selfishness. The longer it takes, the greater the betrayal. He'd done it once before, when the son had reached maturity. His role complete, he had departed. As if that made it any better. He should have stayed away then, but he didn't. Never return, never go back! On the contrary, always go back. If you can bear to.

The second affair, therefore, came as no great surprise. The son had long since given up on the nonsensical childhood fallacy that his parents were no more than his parents. The earlier you're introduced to this cruel fact of life, the better. All children are utterly selfish, and it is not until they have children of their own that they realise it.

The second disappearance left wreckage which he (the grandfather) did nothing to repair. It was less of a surprise, but even more shocking. You get to foul things up once, you don't get to maul the corpse.

No doubt the grandfather thought repair was impossible. He wasn't good with his hands; he couldn't stoop to carve with his own worn-out tools. Not like his own father (the other great-grandfather), the complicated bully. The unfinished carpenter. The misunderstood wife-beater. Nonetheless, there was no need to impose his new joy on everyone else. They did not share it. His arrogant refusal to accept any advice caused a great rift in the already broken family. By not tempering the blow, he had crushed it flat.

The act ended the moral call for endurance. It was then a free-for-all. If the patriarch can leave, then we can all leave. The son didn't blame him for that. In a sense, it had helped cleave his own destiny.

Many years later, the son understood his father (the grandfather) better and was once more able to appreciate the qualified support. By then so much damage had been done to the family that it could only be repaired in patches. Some things remained though, and they again played games together, as he had done when he was a boy.

77 (Sunset Strip)

If you need to strip, do it in the dark.

She (the grandmother) never got over it. Never stopped raging, never stopped blaming 'the other woman', that 'whore'. It would almost have been funny except that it was not. At all.

The son remembered joining the rage once, two voices howling in a gale of tears. She had come to visit and immediately began berating the past.

"He needs to get real…"

Normally he'd have ignored it. The grandmother deserved her rage; she had been wronged. She had heroically tried to hold the grim remains of the family together and essentially driven herself insane in the process. She had, after all, rebuilt herself piece by broken piece. But the cracks still showed and today was not the day for them.

"I've had enough!" he shouted. "I don't want to hear about it any more, I'm sick of it. If you can't talk about something else, then go home. Fuck off."

Not the finest moment, but finer than the madness. That cannot be told here. Not yet.

88 (Two Fat Ladies)

Nearly there (the father, son and holy toast).

One of them came to stay. I wonder if they'll get stuck in the lavatory. A laboratory of age, sample size three. If I'm offensive, then please be offended – I will not be told what I can say by a virtue-signalling ingenue.

Less anger now because there is less of everything, except fear. Still plenty to go round, though.

The price I pay for my intransigence is loneliness. These scattered thoughts, these bone relics of a life.

Bogs

Of all the places in which to die, a toilet is not the one. Of all the toilets in which to die, don't go public. The last thing I can remember is seeing stars and feeling faint. Trying to move this boulder made me feel sorry for Sisyphus. Nothing new there. But then it turned into an out of body experience that I stayed out of. I've been floating here in this stench for 50 years and there is nothing to do except jump out and say, "Poo!" I have a penchant for puns.

Everyone says that there are no such things as ghosts. Of course there aren't, or we'd all have seen one when we were alive. Why would they be so rare? But it's really that we're all quite depressed and don't feel like socialising. I don't get to go out much. All I have to keep me company are the inane doodles of those who feel a presence. You can't really run away with your trousers around your ankles. The ghost of this mass passed. Too much sherry log. I was going to write a story about toilets, but I thought it might be shit.

My favourite piece of graffiti was when someone scrawled 'Why are you here?' whilst having a dump. Why indeed! Surely you can hold on until you get home. In response to this existential enquiry, someone more literally-minded had drawn a table to which people could add a tally. The column headings were Shit, Piss, Smoke and Other. Other had me confused for a while but then somebody helpfully added Wank. Wank was winning. However, I can assure you that this is incorrect data capture!

Clearly Piss is the most common, but it's hard to write while having a slash, and anyway, Wank has more comedic value.

This is not what I call eternity. My haunt name is Bogs. You get given a haunt name at the passing-over parade.

*

A few vital words about statistics. There are plenty more where these came from, but it'll do for now. Correlation is not the same as causation. It might be, but it might not. This is obvious if you think about it, but often we don't. We're wired not to. Evolution makes us look for patterns and associations that aren't there, just to be on the safe side. Best to assume those glints in the darkness are the eyes of a savage beast. Assume they're glints of starlight and you're going to look pretty daft when it pounces. You'll look fairly cool if they are indeed just glints of starlight, but that isn't how evolution works.

There are three types of correlation: genuine causation, coincidence, and ghost correlation. Causation predicts the future, coincidence does not. Ghost correlation predicts the future, but you don't know why.

The first is easy and the link is real. For example, young male drivers and accidents. There is clear, proven correlation over time which will continue into the future. The EU, in one of its less pertinent judgements, decided that it had nothing to do with being a young male but actually to do with aggressive and inexperienced driving. True, but hardly the point. Anyway, it's a sad fact and will continue to be so. Just take a look at the mortality curve split by gender: there's still a sickening hump at around 17 years old for the boys. Of course, correlation can be weak or strong. No one is saying that all young male drivers are testosterone-fuelled dickheads, but on average they are consistently bad. If you don't like that example then fine, you can have being kicked in the balls and pain. The link is very real.

Fake correlation, or coincidence, happens all the time. If you think of all the bazillions of possible combinations of things out there, some are just going to happen at once. Apparently enough random things happened once to create (I mean spontaneously erupt) a protocell. Weird. One example of fake correlation was eating cheese, and death by strangulation. I say *was* because it won't be any more. But for a time, the world threw up a precise correlation between noshing down on cheddar and being choked to death. Plot the lines on a graph and they're on top of each other, like two snakes shagging. Clearly this is baloney and doesn't predict the future.

The other third kind, ghost correlation, is more subtle. Here there is a genuine connection between a predictor and an outcome, but there's a missing link. Take listening to Mozart and having a clever baby. Bull. Shit. Mozart is no doubt a musical genius, but there's no way he makes your kid clever. Nonetheless, there appears to be a sustainable correlation. Perhaps the kinds of people who listen to classical music are the kinds of people who have clever babies; perhaps higher socio-economic groups tend to listen to it more. Who knows? But it is highly unlikely to be down to Wolfgang. If everyone had speakers implanted in their wombs during pregnancy in order to replicate this effect, it would disappear. It's not actually called ghost correlation, as far as I know, but it should be. Give me some latitude.

Incidentally, you might have heard imbeciles saying that anyone can be Mozart if they just practice for 10,000 hours. This is absolutely not true. It's deterministic fascism. But we digress.

The reason we're talking about correlation and causation is that I have a theory. Whilst I admit that I have become rather fixated on toilets of late, I believe there is a direct link between divorce rates and *en suite* bathrooms. I believe that *en suite* bathrooms are destroying marriage. They are corroding its very fabric, just as limescale corrodes them. Bitterness only corrodes the vessel that holds it, but *en suites* are less selective. Their splash is universal; they are the work of the devil.

I need hardly go into any more detail, but I will.

While performing one's nightly ablutions, a degree of decorum is required. Some things are best done in private, discretely. Shamefully, even. Bathroom rituals should be neither seen nor heard. The slate of fantasy should never be wiped clean.

No one wants to hear *Prince Charming* let rip; nobody wants to see *Snow White* taking a leak. A tsunami of urine gushing like the Niagara Falls over the abysmal toilet rim, the thunderous splat of turd hitting porcelain; the cataclysmic flush, the token rinse of cold, clammy, dead hands. And then, wafting, dreamlike, into the boudoir.

"Now lick this."

It doesn't exactly get me in the mood.

I don't need a string quartet and candles, but I'd rather my lover hadn't just been for a swim in the River Styx. A bit of romance would be nice. If you don't feel for it, you don't kneel for it. The tainting of physical passion in this disgusting fashion has led directly to the increase in divorce rates: correlation and unassailable causation. The only people who stay married now are the ones who enjoy hearing their spouses evacuating in front of them. Or live in an old house. If you want to stay married, buy an old house. Let me come and stay there. Please.

It's rather like replicating the festival experience in your own bedroom but without bands, food, or drugs. Imagine going to a festival and only having the toilets. Minimalist. I'm sure some people would still go. Shy bowel, my arse! More like fly bowel. Bowel that doesn't want to be invaded by a legion of germs that you can actually feel oozing up your legs, burrowing into your skin. Hanging with my legs akimbo over a mountain of bog roll. Yippee! Don't think I'll be reading a book in there, thanks. I would literally rather crap myself than use a festival toilet. You don't have to believe me, but there were witnesses. They shared the car home.

Crude horrors aside, I also believe that the true picture is much more sinister. *En suites* were not created in response to customer demand. The very opposite is true. Companies created the demand and then lied to customers about their needs. It's how the system works. Why does anybody want a bog in their bedroom?

There is a dark cabal of globalist power-mongers (The Nonsense) who have secretly been plotting this for generations. They own all the building companies – they own everything. I recall going to a relatively posh house in the late-'80s and being astounded that they had three toilets. Nobody had *en suites* 40 years ago. Suddenly they were everywhere, like triffids, Alien shapeshifters ruthlessly destroying all that is sacred. They want to undermine marriage and all Abrahamic religions in order to spread their satanic neoliberal globalism. We must fight!

*

After the *en suites* came the toilet wars. Classic playbook. Suddenly, no one could talk about anything else. The nappy of The Nonsense-owned media was saturated with it. There was a guerilla group called Rage Against the Latrine whose protests included public defecation. They had a point: the lack of provision is a national disgrace. But that's no way to get people onside. For a while, there were a range of glittering new toilets provided, under emergency legislation. It was important to keep the population in a state of fear and emergency. The Crapping Crisis. These latrines had doors that opened automatically, and a choice of music. My own favourite was the *Blue Danube*. Obviously there needed to be a time limit, otherwise people would use them for shagging in and sleeping. Or both.

The units worked out at around £1 million a cubicle, the cost of which was borne by the taxpayer. Most of the profit went to friends and relatives of the government minister who signed off on the deal. Unfortunately, there were several incidents of the doors opening prematurely, which gave rise to a new pressure group supporting chronic constipation sufferers: We Shall Not Be Moved.

The Nonsense then funded aggressive trans groups to protest the lack of suitable toilet provision. Waving placards, saying 'We Demand To Be Turd', these protesters regularly clashed with TERFs who were protesting about the very opposite. Most trans people didn't give a flying fuck about toilets; they had bigger fish to fry. Most biological women just didn't want biological men using their toilets because men stink. Hard to argue with that. Maybe it should be the test. I must write to the Olympics committee.

By making the public believe this was a single-issue movement, The Nonsense was able to divide and conquer, sow hatred.

Don't look over here at us feasting on the flesh of your children's future, look over there! Get rid of those bastards and it will all be fine. By targeting the traditional views of men, women and marriage, these nefarious monsters were seeking to reduce the global population. It all made perfect sense.

In one Californian town there were 12 different toilet varieties. Locals who had lived there for generations were being 'forced out' to make way for aggressive toilet developers. By forced out I mean they selfishly chose to sell their houses at a premium to incomers, but that isn't the point. They had no choice but to sell, once the streets were overrun by bogs which stood empty half the year. Holiday thrones. You could even buy your own gold-plated beach pissoir if you cared to. A group of vigilante arsonists called Feel The Burn began torching them. They didn't have houses they could sell to developers so were complaining about the fact it had happened. I have a lot of sympathy with them. There are false rumours that one exploded after it was lit up too soon following a visit from a stupendously odorous gentleman in Suffolk.

It all got a bit out of hand. Now that they have seemingly milked this opportunity dry, The Nonsense will move on to other areas of discord. I fear that they are creating a plague. This will be secretly released in festival toilets to wipe out the young! They've tried it before for gay people, they can do it again. I must stop them; I must save the world.

No one will believe me.

*

No will believe me because it is utter crap! I made it all up. There is unspeakable horror everywhere, at all levels. It is mercifully rare, but that's all you hear about if that's all you listen out for. This fiddle only plays one tune. Every conspiracy theory can be explained away by vested interests, power and greed. A government that can't even cover up a blowjob can somehow cover up a moon landing. Sure it can! Every explanation becomes a new conspiracy theory. So chose the easiest. Occam knew best. Actually, he probably didn't, and most people ignore the fact that the simplest explanation is only more desirable if it works. Be that as it may, but if you don't know, then why not pick the most plausible. Corruption rules. You've got to feel it, man.

I met Satan himself once, at the passing-over parade. I was being escorted by a chubby celestial being, the angel of the lard. The ceremony was all a bit glum and there was a lot of hanging around. Satan and I didn't speak for long, it was more of a brush past. But I can tell you with some authority that he doesn't even like the blood of babies. He prefers claret.

The part about *en suites* is true though, I am sure of it. A far better use of the extractor fan is to rip out the *en suite* and create a pipe smoking room.

The Divorce Clinic

1 Divorce with reasonable people

"Good morning, Mr and Mrs Brownlow, it's a pleasure to meet you. I'm Jane Saunders, we spoke briefly on the phone. I wish it were in more pleasant circumstances, but we'll do our best. Please let me introduce my ex-husband, Clifford. He is mostly busy on the technical side of things but likes to meet our new clients in person."

Clifford judged that shaking hands was probably not required and nodded in a friendly fashion. It was important to get a handle on new business at an early stage so that nobody wasted time. Time wasn't money, nothing so vulgar. But still, there was only so much of it to go round. Demand for their services was reassuringly high and there was no great need to tout. Having him here also made the obvious point that amicable divorce was eminently possible, in the right circumstances. She and Clifford were divorced, but they happily ran a successful business.

"As we discussed, our aim is to make this painful process as straightforward as possible. This is just an initial conversation, and I'm really pleased that you were able to come in together. That is really quite essential. We won't charge for this preliminary session and of course it's up to you whether you proceed. No grin, no fee!"

They had set up the Divorce Clinic around five years ago following their own unnecessarily bruising experience. Since then, they had moved into other product areas, including prenuptials, postnuptials, term marriages, and a renewals process. Business was booming.

The entire point of the Divorce Clinic was to avoid lawyers, who were indeed the rapacious vultures that everyone thought they were. It was a stereotype because it was true. They fuelled conflict and fed like vultures on the corpse of a marriage, setting one contestant against the other until there was nothing left. Sometimes the two lawyers feasting at the throats of their clients employed a third to mediate! Jane and Clifford had endured precisely this experience. They ended up sacking both lawyers, settling on the mediated document, and doing the court paperwork themselves. Ridiculous.

It was almost self-explanatory. They aimed to produce a satisfactory outcome at a fraction of the cost. And, more importantly, they aimed to maintain a good relationship between the plaintiffs. Or rather the non-plaintiffs, at least until lawyers got involved. A happy divorce was almost as important as a happy marriage.

Jane continued, explaining this to the Brownlows:

"You see, now that our esteemed leaders in Westminster have finally modernised divorce law, the whole issue of 'grounds for divorce' is an irrelevance. How on earth it has taken 50 years to get to this point, God only knows. The worst thing about the entire process were the appalling 'reasons' that the petitioner had to give. These were distasteful in the extreme, preposterous, and caused huge distress at the most awful time. At last, people are finally being treated as adults. You can get divorced simply because you want to. Neither partner has the right to refuse, and it is an outrage that they ever could."

"What about in sickness and in health?" said Mrs Brownlow.

"Till death us do part?" added her husband.

Clifford chipped in with his prepared speech. He quite enjoyed this section.

"Well yes, laudable sentiments, of course! Very biblical and quaint. We all get married believing in these colossal pledges. Well, most of us do. But the problem is that we are making a lifelong commitment without the maturity or self-knowledge to do so. It's all marvellous and romantic; we would all love our marriages to last for ever. But sadly, we are often attributing a permanent state to temporary emotions. If that works out then happy days, if it does not then unfortunately our days become much less happy. We have one life to live, that is all."

His ex-wife continued:

"When we got married," said Jane, motioning towards Clifford, "we had no doubts at all. We were in love and stayed blissfully happy for over 10 years. Unfortunately, cracks, both figurative and literal, started to appear. Mercifully we now don't need to go into those!"

"There is no longer a need to list my manifold faults in a legal document," added Clifford.

"Quite so," continued Jane. "Basically, you don't have to stay together if you don't want to. Clifford and I are still the very best of friends, but we do not want to be married to each other. That's the simple and bald truth of the matter. We both think that we had a successful marriage rather than a failed one. Others can think what they like."

"Well, when you put it like that," pondered Mr Brownlow.

"We do still love each other, in a way," said Mrs Brownlow.

"Of course you do! And that is wonderful," said Jane. "This process cannot possibly work if the protagonists are not reasonable people who recognise that things have gone wrong. It is very important that you don't rush into any decision. And it is critical that you don't fall out, particularly since there are children involved. So much devastation is caused by marital debris, and it is really quite unnecessary. We have very firm guidelines on dealing with children in the aftermath."

"We'll go into much more detail at future discussions, of course," said Clifford. "Our basic approach is to move entirely at your pace. We have a fixed fee, which includes 10 hours of conversations like this. If more are required, then they can be added at a significant discount. If we get to the point when no further progress is possible, then you are entitled to a full refund. This is extremely rare once we begin."

"What makes us wholly different to all other providers in this field is that we aim to avoid divorce. Our reconciliation process will uncover what is at the root of the problem, if that isn't already very clear. If we can avoid divorce, then that's a good thing. If we cannot, then it will at least be as amicable as possible," said Jane.

"But if we stay together, you don't get paid!" said Mr Brownlow.

"Well, you are of course entitled to a full refund. But this has yet to happen! Our experience so far is that the reconciliation process is so well received by people that they are happy to forgo our very reasonable fee. They consider it money well spent! It is a mere fraction of the cost of divorce, which in the end usually means both parties splitting their joint assets in half," added Jane.

Clifford added some analytical content. He felt that a pie chart was an entirely suitable visualisation of the divorce process.

"Generally speaking, around a quarter of our clients end up staying together; half get divorced without any acrimony, and unfortunately the rest don't fit our profile. We don't embark on a journey of mutual discovery with them; we bid them unwelcome at an early stage. As Jane mentioned, we can only work with couples who are open to being civilised. We are a baboon-free zone. Where there's a will, there's a way!"

"If the divorce does proceed, you will find that our charges are extremely competitive. If we cannot arrive at an amicable settlement, you can take your business elsewhere, with no hard feelings. This is most unusual."

"I certainly wouldn't want to use Bastard and Prick, like my friend," said Mrs Brownlow. "They were awful. And her husband's lawyer was Mr Claw, horrendous character. All they did was write expensive letters to each other for no apparent reason, and fuel dissent. It cost them tens of thousands and ended up in a court battle. Totally unnecessary."

Mr Brownlow nodded in agreement.

"Absolutely," said Jane. "We'd be happy to start the process now, since you're here, but usually it's best if you go away and reflect. Our secretary will be happy to arrange the first session, and you can just pay on the day. No paperwork required – we're not a big fan of unnecessary contracts. Of course, if you prefer, then we can have one drawn up, but it's basically a waste of time. You're free to stop the process at any time."

"Oh, and one other thing!" said Clifford. "It's quite unusual, but you can always remarry! Some of our clients have secured an amicable divorce and then realised, to their horror, that it was the worst decision of their lives. They, to some extent, stumble into divorce, which seems like the best idea at the time, but then as age and wisdom replace impulse, they recognise that the forces which drove them apart are unequal to the force of reuniting! In other words, give divorce a whirl and see how it suits you."

Jane sighed. Clifford always added this part, and she felt it was taking hope too far.

"This is quite rare though, and it's best to be certain you're doing the right thing," she said.

"As certain as you were about getting married in the first place, anyway!" quipped Clifford.

Mr Brownlow chuckled slightly. They were shown out of the door.

"Well, they seem fairly pleasant. Our kind of people," said Clifford

"Yes, indeed. I'm not so sure about the next couple, she sounded a bit fraught on the phone. I'm not entirely sure that they will show up," said Jane.

"Oh well, then we can put our feet up for an hour."

2 Divorce with unreasonable people

Clifford was surprised that they had come at all, such was the evident underlying hostility. Introductions had gone reasonably well, albeit rather low on smiles. Now Mr Wilson bristled with indignation as his wife calmly outlined the reasons for their visit. After gradually changing hue from pasty white to gammon pink, he finally burst out of his skin, like a sausage.

"You shagged the milkman!"

"Really? Is that that still a thing?" said Clifford.

"Are you taking the piss?" enquired Mr Wilson.

His wife explained, "It's The Milkman, with capitals. He is called that because he keeps a cow in his field. And no, I haven't shagged him. But I suppose I might at some point."

"What!" shouted Mr Wilson, standing up.

"Look, please, Mrs and Mr Wilson, this really isn't going to help," said Jane, hoping to reduce the room temperature. "We're not here to apportion blame or arbitrate a slanging match. You are not yet our clients and we are advising nothing. After I spoke to Mrs Wilson a few days ago, I was under the impression that you both wished to attend and that discussions were likely to be constructive. Clearly that isn't the case."

She and her ex-husband were both prone to snap judgements and really didn't need to be chasing business. Clifford decided to wrap things up quickly.

"This was only a preliminary discussion, which as you know we're happy to provide for free. It was essentially to gain an understanding of whether our approach is likely to be of benefit. It is quite clear that, currently, it is not. Do feel free to come back when you're able to be in the same room as each other without hurling abuse."

"I'm not listening to any more of this shit," announced Mr Wilson, slamming the door on his way out.

His soon-to-be ex-wife sat quietly.

"I'm sorry if I was a little blunt, Mrs Wilson, but I don't think your husband is quite on the same page as you," remarked Clifford.

"No, it's fair to say he isn't. His bilious micro-rages are a large part of the problem."

"I probably shouldn't say this, but I can quite see why you are taking the line that you are," said Jane. "Do you have any fears for your safety? If you're concerned in any way about your husband's ongoing reaction, then we're able to refer you to some protection, or accommodation at very reasonable rates."

"Don't be ridiculous! That is hardly necessary. Brian is harmless enough; he just goes off on one from time to time and won't accept that I simply don't love him any more. He may come round. If not, then I'll have to force the issue. I feel awful about it but being stuck in this loveless marriage is even more awful. I'm probably being selfish."

"Perhaps. Or perhaps it is selfish of him not to see it. Either way, it is enormously sad and there is no easy way out of the situation. We wish you all the best," said Clifford.

Jane stood to see Mrs Wilson out.

"Can I still use your services on my own?"

"I'm afraid not. We have a very niche offering that just doesn't suit everyone. There are plenty more adversarial options available though, if it comes to that. I've heard that Bastard and Prick are effective, albeit quite expensive. I do hope that things work out. If you do return, then I'm afraid we'll have to charge for any future sessions."

3 Prenuptial agreement

Another popular service the Divorce Clinic provided was the writing of prenuptials. These were still not legally binding, but effectively they were. With courts overrun and underfunded, anything that could speed up the process tended to be gratefully received. Besides which, the process of establishing a prenuptial agreement ensured that only reasonable people got married in the first place.

Data for the prenuptial agreement was gathered via sometimes elaborate discussions and also through a questionnaire, which

Clifford collated and analysed. They generally found that these discussions either purged the concerns of the betrothed or drove them apart. Either way, a very useful process.

You could find out a great deal about someone once you started discussing money.

The agreements were immensely thorough and covered all aspects of current income and wealth. These were quite often lied about, but not nearly so often as during divorce without an agreement in place. Passions tended to be rather less nurturing at that stage. As well as clearly identifying those assets which each party took into the marriage, detailed provision was made for future changes.

Some of details were dry, but the main areas were standard. Obviously, people could select 'not applicable' if they wanted to kick the can down the road. While most clients were primarily concerned with financial matters, the clinic had also found that some other areas benefited from greater clarity. The line of questioning was intentionally provocative.

Income: how will this be shared? How much of any future increases in salary is your spouse entitled to? How much of your future income is down to the loving caress of your partner? Surely most of it would have happened anyway and is down to your own efforts? Half? Why is half the maximum if you're just a lucky, lazy slob and your spouse did all the hard work? A third? Will you transfer half of your salary each month into their account? Both your salaries into an increasingly anachronistic joint account? Needs talking about.

Children: if one spouse gives up more of their work to look after children, how will this be quantified? Will you pay them an annual salary for childcare duties? If so, what duties will you still have?

Household chores: a minefield! It was amazing how sexist people were. Some didn't mind a bit of harmless differentiation. Others did.

Wealth: your spouse borrowed a chunk of cash from her parents for your first house. Should he/she therefore own a higher proportion of it? How about if 20 years hence that chunk of cash has quadrupled in value? Who pays the mortgage? Should they get a bigger share? If you don't care, that's fine, you don't have to.

Habits: this was always a good one. If nothing else, it served to flush away any unspoken resentment. Jane recalled one woman who had called off a marriage because her prospective husband refused to stop whistling. Yes, she could have lived with it, but why should she? Jane was in full agreement. See if he carries on whistling quite so much when you dump him. Talking of which, another had complained about her partner bursting into the bathroom for 'a dump' when she was having a bath. Jane thought that this was punishable by death, let alone calling off a wedding.

Sex: most people put 'not applicable' here. Or perhaps a broad brush 'no issues'. After all, sex is fine and dandy when you're young; it can largely be taken as read. However, there were some areas that could be addressed, if so desired. Once, Clifford had been unable to stop himself laughing out loud when a young woman in ankle socks had claimed she and her fiancé were saving themselves for their wedding night.

In any case, most couples found it a useful exercise.

*

Some couples, of course, didn't want to go near a prenuptial agreement – it wasn't romantic. True enough. Having your wife take away your house and your kids while she fucked her new partner in your old bedroom wasn't vastly romantic either. Nor was trying to make ends meet while your apparently charming young husband served a prison sentence for grievous bodily harm. Other scenarios are available, but you catch the drift. Perhaps it was worth spending a bit of money facilitating some honest conversations, before you lashed 10 times that up the wall for one day of feeding your fat, posturing relatives.

A typical conversation might run something like this:

"We wouldn't do that! We would never behave like that!"

"You wouldn't now, no, of course not. Circumstances can change, though. How would you feel if Dave had three mistresses? How would Dave feel if you were an alcoholic?"

"But we will make vows. We don't break vows."

"No one intends to. The path to divorce is littered with unfulfilled promises."

"We would never, ever cheat on each other, we know that."

"It's not all about adultery. The vow that most people break is the one about cherishing. Easy to forget, and very hard to define."

And so on. This was not about scaring people away – it was about raising issues that really ought to be addressed in advance. It was madness to leave discussions about a marriage until after the marriage. You need an exit strategy! Besides, if your meringue wedding can't survive a few tough questions, then maybe you should call it off.

Naturally, some couples didn't want to be exposed to this kind of gritty reality, but with half of marriages now ending in divorce, to ignore it was naive. The picture wasn't quite so bleak, of course. As ever, the devil was the detail. The headline figure that 'Half of all marriages end in divorce!' included people who had been divorced several times or were divorced because of violence or were happily divorced after 30 years spent raising two well-adjusted children. Marriage remained a glorious institution for the majority.

But not for all. It was important, and highly beneficial, to air these issues before the blissful ceremony took place.

4 Postnuptial agreement

This was essentially a pre-arranged divorce settlement while married. Clients were advised to write one before having children, or if financial circumstances changed. The fact that you won't agree to one could be considered grounds for divorce! Not that you need grounds any more.

Jane described it in pragmatic terms: if you were not married, would you now be planning your wedding day? If not, then why are you still married? Endurance isn't a good reason. Entrapment is even worse.

Very often, the postnuptial agreement was the same as the prenuptial agreement but with the benefit of maturity and hindsight. Older people were less likely to ignore the sex section when it could no longer be taken as read and was less of an all-consuming hobby. There were some interesting concepts that could be fleshed out when gazing into the crack of doom.

For example, the clinic had adopted the term Omega Shag that referred to your last act of sexual intercourse. Teenagers were obsessed with losing their virginity; perhaps older people should reflect on when they might be forced to regain it. When do you expect to become celibate? Was this acceptable to both parties? Would one, or both, of you be prepared to accept a degree of latitude as far as fidelity was concerned? Has your once rampant libido ebbed away into an occasional flutter and, if so, does this matter?

Similarly, the Fellatio Ratio spoke for itself. As did the Clitmus Test.

5 Term Marriages

Jane and Clifford were explaining their most radical product offering to the recently engaged Tom Jobbing and Maggie Blowers. Tom was a bored jewellery shop manager who did pottery in his spare time and had curly hair. Maggie was an accountant who also enjoyed animal husbandry and kickboxing (occasionally at the same time if cornered by cattle). She had a very important job but didn't go on about it. Both looked and seemed lovely.

"This is probably our most controversial suggestion to date, so please forgive us if it isn't something you'd naturally be drawn to," said Jane. "But since you've had the foresight to accept our prenuptial services, we'd like to share it with you. For term marriages, a prenuptial agreement is a *sine qua non*. Full and frank feedback will be much appreciated."

"In essence, we are proposing fixed term marriages rather than the traditional whole life arrangement," she continued. "You agree to be married for a specified period, at the end of which you can either renew, free of charge, or trigger a divorce, according to the terms previously agreed. It enables some couples to, as it were, try out marriage to see if it suits them. Given that it is the biggest decision you'll make in your life, we feel it makes sense to consider a less than forever arrangement. At least in the first instance."

"Sort of suck it and see," added Clifford.

Ignoring him, Jane carried on. "Though any term is available, we think that the one, three, five, ten and twenty-year options cover most eventualities. One year is hardly worth the bother and few people take it; 20 years is quite a sentence but seems to be a tipping point. It's not very popular, but some people think that it gets you past the children growing up."

"Surely that defeats the whole point of marriage?" said Tom.

"Well yes, to some extent," said Jane. "It certainly flies in the face of the traditional Christian view of things. But that isn't for everyone. Why should you be bound by conventions dating back to a millennia-old patriarchy? If that still speaks to you, then of course, that's fantastic, but I'm sure you'd agree that the world was quite different then. I notice from our discussions that neither of you have a strong religious affiliation and are unlikely to marry in church."

"That's true. We're hoping to get married at a Roman site nearby, between a pair of 500-year-old oak trees, in a quasi-Druidic style," said Maggie.

"Oh yes, I think I know that field," said Clifford. "Incidentally, I applaud your decision to invent a new surname rather than the pretentious and farcically indecisive double-barrelled nonsense."

"Thanks. Our existing surnames didn't really gel, and I don't have any grandparents I need to immortalise. Tom does, but we've agreed that we'll use their surname as a middle name for our firstborn. If we don't have a firstborn, then the family name will die out soon enough anyway."

Jane continued, "Just to clarify, at the end of the fixed term we can automatically renew the policy if you prefer, but we strongly advise going through a full in-person renewal process. This consists of a thorough discussion of your performances during the marriage so far, and whether each of you has pulled their weight, so to speak. In your case, Maggie has agreed to bring a higher degree of financial security and Tom, a more supportive role – lifting things and so on. Has this happened to your mutual satisfaction? We could in theory have an auto divorce option for people who were committed to partial commitment. Although no one has selected that to date."

Clifford took up the baton. "If you're both happy at the end of your trial period then that's terrific, you can simply renew for the same term or change to a new length. You can also revert to a whole life policy if you wish. If you're not happy, then you can divorce – the paperwork is already virtually complete. The real test of a marriage is whether you're choosing to stay together or not. Remove that choice and therein lies misery. As with all our services, this is about trying to offer sensible options to civilised people. Beware the divorce lawyers."

"Of course, this isn't yet legally enforceable, but we think precedents should be set – it helps manage expectations. There will always be adversarial legal hawks who want to stoke the smoke of separation. They are best avoided," said Jane.

Tom and Maggie seemed open to the novelty of this idea and said they would think about it. They were pleased to have finalised the prenuptial agreement in an earlier session. Reassuringly, that process hadn't thrown up any clangers.

Clifford was also keen to tell them about his pet side project, the marriage predictor. Using well established cost modelling techniques it was quite straightforward to give a length of marriage forecast, if you considered divorce to be an 'accident'. Risk factors such as age, wealth, health, previous experience, interests, attitude to various triggering events and so on, were already captured through the detailed questionnaire that they had used for the prenuptial agreement. It was simply a matter of running it through the algorithm and out pops your length of marriage forecast!

"It's a bit like being told the sex of your baby: appeals to some, not others. Of course, it's rather less accurate than that. Models are never definite things; statistically likely is by no means the same as certain. It's amazing how many people don't realise that."

"I'm not sure," said Tom. "I suppose it might be fun!"

"We'll let you know," said Maggie. "Hardly worth bothering with the marriage at all if your prediction is only six weeks."

Clifford smiled. "Forecast not prediction," he corrected mildly. "Having met you, I'd say that is extremely unlikely. Besides which, estimates at the extremes are quite flaky – less than a year and 20-plus years are the outer limits."

Jane wrapped up the session. "Just let us know whether you'd like to consider the fixed term marriage option. If not, then it has been a pleasure working with you. I sincerely hope that you never need your agreement and wish you both the very best of luck."

The newly betrothed couple beamed, shook hands, and walked out together. They held each other in a gesture of informed innocence.

"Love's young dream," sighed Clifford.

"But for a moment, our own," replied Jane.

www.ingramcontent.com/pod-product-compliance
Lightning Source LLC
Chambersburg PA
CBHW020910180626
46816CB00007BA/2335